CLICHÉ

EPISODES ONE, TWO, AND THREE

CLICHÉ: EPISODES ONE, TWO, AND THREE
Copyright © 2020 by Jeff Menapace

CLICHÉ: EPISODE ONE
Copyright © 2017 by Jeff Menapace

CLICHÉ: EPISODE TWO
Copyright © 2018 by Jeff Menapace

CLICHÉ: EPISODE THREE
Copyright © 20209 by Jeff Menapace

Published by Mind Mess Press
All Rights Reserved

ISBN: 9798621052355

All rights reserved. Without limiting the rights under copyright above, no part of this publication may be reproduced, stored in or introduced into any retrieval system, or transmitted in any form or by any means (electronic, mechanical, photocopying, recording or otherwise) without the prior written permission of the copyright owner or the publisher of this book.

This book is a work of fiction. Names, characters, places, and incidents are a product of the author's imagination or are used fictitiously. Any resemblance to actual events, locales, or persons, living or dead, is coincidental.

CLICHÉ

EPISODES ONE, TWO, AND THREE

JEFF MENAPACE

2020

CLICHÉ

IN NUMB, CALVIN COURT USED TO JOKE THAT HIS LIFE WAS A SERIES OF CLICHÉS. HE HAD NO IDEA…

Welcome to The Track. An elite club for members whose depraved desires run to the extreme. A place where you can bet on a pony and see how long he can survive…in a deadly scenario decided by a simple spin of the wheel.

Step right up.

This series of shorts is a follow-up to the novel NUMB. However, it can just as easily be enjoyed as a standalone series.

CLICHE
EPISODE ONE

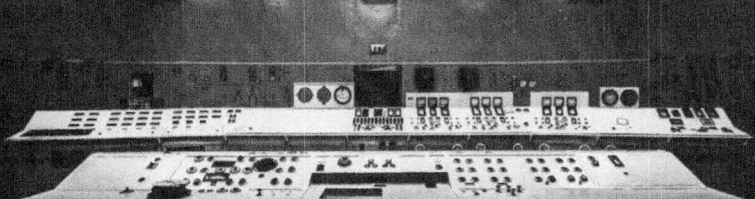

THE TRACK

The elite room known to its members as The Track was located not in the penthouse of the mile-high building, but in the basement.

Access came through endlessly dank corridors of concrete; through locked gates, metal detectors, and X-ray screening every few hundred feet, overseen not by fat men on minimum wage waiting for their coffee and smoke break, but by fit, imposing men, attired in dress more fitting to a government worker than a simple turnkey.

Through the endless corridors until you finally arrived at The Track.

Curiously, no guard waited outside the entrance, only a small metal panel to the right of the door, the panel not asking for a thumbprint or mag card or password, but a retinal scan. A retinal scan with a clever safeguard installed: If you'd managed to make your way to the basement floor; conned—or killed—your way past the guards; and then fancied yourself brazen enough to place your eye up to that little metal panel next to the door, a sudden twelve-inch steel spike was your reward.

Angela Thorne was not worried about a twelve-inch spike in the eye. True, this was her first time at The Track, but she'd been invited by the elite. After years of waiting and proving herself, she'd finally been invited to step through the door and into a den of men and women whose lust for money was only matched by the means by which it was attained.

The hunt. It was all about the hunt.

Of course the hunt itself was not immune from stagnancy. Like the addict who incessantly chases the thrill of their first high, so too did these elite members of the organization pursue new methods to carry out the hunt. Riskier methods. Really, really fucked-up methods.

Angela Thorne and really, really fucked-up got along swimmingly.

It was the reason she'd finally been invited to The Track. That and she had one hell of a pony.

Calvin was his name.

. . .

Despite being invited and displaying the same lack of empathy and compassion as the rest of the table, Angela *was* still a rookie at The Track. A little hazing was to be expected.

"Ahhh…free money," Tom Neil said with a condescending little grin as Angela took a seat at the table.

"Cute," was all Angela said.

To the onlooker, it might have been a boardroom meeting. Spacious office. Big rectangular table in the center. Senior-most members of The Track at the head of that table.

That's where the comparisons stopped.

Behind those senior-most members was a wall of technology that would make the brightest at MIT blush. Everything the table coveted was documented, tracked, and projected on that wall. The hunt was on that wall.

"So…Angela, I hear you've got quite the pony." Robert Stiles. *The* senior-most member, seated at the very head of the table. Seventy, gaunt, and gray. Immaculately dressed. Billionaire.

All eyes fell on Angela. Some—those of men—lingered longer than others. Members of The Track were members of The Track because they needed more—needed the hunt. Atrocity in the guise of sport. But sex *was* still sex, and Angela Thorne was as fine a candidate as they got.

"I like to think so," Angela replied. She brushed a lock of long dark hair behind her ear, the gesture accentuating her beauty. She was not too proud to use her looks to obtain what she wanted. She did, in fact, relish the chance—men or women so easily swayed by sex appeal deserved to be taken for the suckers they were. And perhaps that sucker was here, would allow her to double down on her bets after some harmless flirting—assuming she got a favorable spin of the wheel, that is.

"Then without further ado," Robert Stiles replied. He pulled a remote control from beneath the desk and ordered it to be handed down the table to Angela.

Angela took it, pressed the proper buttons, and "spun the wheel." Hundreds of options flashed on one of the bigger screens along the wall, like data being processed by a computer too fast for the naked eye to catch. When it stopped its spin and displayed the day's clichéd scenario to be, Angela could not help but smirk.

Tom Neil caught Angela's subtle delight. Such confidence for a rookie. He didn't like it.

"Feeling confident already, are you?" he said. His tone was more challenging than courteous.

Angela only smiled in return.

"Well, maybe you're confident enough to double down with me then," he said. "What do you say?"

Angela kept on smiling. An offer to double down right off the bat, and without so much as a bat of the eye. Quite the opposite, in fact: a blow to the male ego.

Or maybe not so opposite: sex and male pride were both governed by lack of rational thinking, as far as Angela was concerned.

"Sure," Angela said. "You're on."

They arranged the bet.

Finished, Tom Neil sat back and grinned. "Like I said the moment you walked in here: free money. I've got two hunters under contract with me for this scenario. They've collected on over *fifty percent* of their gigs since I've had them. No way your pony gets out alive, rookie."

The table murmured.

Still smiling, Angela nodded as if conceding to Tom's stronger hand. In reality, she was placating the hell out of him.

"Just a quick FYI," she said, gesturing to the screen that displayed the day's scenario. "Crazy as it sounds, this is the precise cliché where I initially hooked my pony."

Although everyone at the table had already read the screen, they glanced at it once more in unison, Angela's confidence in her pony for the day's cliché demanding a second look.

BAR FIGHT, the screen read, larger than life.

"Talk about beginner's luck, huh?" Angela said.

Tom only sucked his teeth and said, "We'll see, *rookie*."

"Okay, that's enough of that, you two," Robert Stiles said. "Everyone else, start placing your bets and getting your business in order. If you've got hunters for this scenario like Tom, contact them and see whether they're interested—wait, what's the cap on this one?"

"Three hunters," a member in the middle of the table replied.

"You using both for this, Tom?" Stiles asked him.

"Damn right," he replied, then glared Angela's way.

Angela winked at him.

"Okay, so only room for one more hunter. If you're interested, make it happen."

The table pulled out smartphones, laptops, tablets. Started doing their thing.

"Angela," Stiles said, "your boy as good as you say he is?"

"Calvin? Let's just say that he's been in far more precarious situations than a bar fight. He's not always pretty, but he is very, *very* hard to kill."

"You are aware that such a prospect is possible—sometimes even encouraged. If someone expires—hunter, pony, even an actor or an extra—so be it. It only stops when the director calls it a day on the set."

"I know the rules," she replied.

Robert Stiles nodded once and pulled out his phone. He placed a sizeable bet on Calvin.

Tom Neil frowned when he heard it. Angela winked at him again.

THE SET

I'm on a bar stool.

I'm sitting on a bar stool in a bar, yet I don't remember coming here.

I don't remember...I don't remember anything.

Am I drunk? I don't *feel* drunk. There's no drink in front of me. Maybe I just finished one and the bartender took it away.

"Excuse me?" I call to the bartender.

He comes over. Fiftyish. Thick handlebar mustache. Greasy dark hair parted down the middle. White shirt and white apron. He looks more like an old-time barber than a bartender to me.

"Another?" he says.

"Another? So I *have* been drinking?"

He makes a face like he just smelled a fart. "*What?*"

"How long have I been here?" I ask.

He makes a swift cutting gesture across his neck. "Okay, you're cut off, partner."

"Wait, I don't—I'm not drunk. I genuinely want to know how long I've been here. I can't seem to remember anything." I shake my head hard. "Jesus, I don't even remember my fucking *name*."

He makes the fart face again, shakes his head and walks away.

I look around. The bar is like something out of a movie. What do they call them? Honkytonks? Country music on the jukebox. Confederate flag behind the bar. Neon beer signs everywhere. Cowboy hats and boots on nearly every patron, even the women. Flannel and denim for miles.

Not a single black guy or girl in sight. If John Wayne parked himself on a stool next to me right now, I wouldn't blink twice.

Why the *hell* am I in a place like this?

Someone takes a stool next to me. Not John Wayne. He's a big guy, though. Thick wrists and hands resting on the bar. He's wearing—wait for it—a flannel shirt, jeans, and a cowboy hat. Two of the knuckles on his right hand are bulbous and knobby. His thumb is crooked. This tells me he's busted his hand plenty of times before in fights, and that he's a righty.

Why do I know this? Better question: Why was it instinctive for me to look for it?

I risk a subtle glance towards his face and am not surprised to see a crooked nose and a long white scar slicing through a bushy black eyebrow.

The jacked-up right hand, the bent nose, the scars. No stranger to violence, this guy. And that's fine; it's his life.

What's *not* fine is that there are a lot of empty bar stools along the bar and he chose one right next to me.

"How's it going?" I say to him. My tone is low and even. Respectful more than friendly.

He turns only his head to me, looks me up and down. "Yankee boy, are you?" His voice is deep and rough with a southern drawl, of course.

I look myself up and down too. I'm wearing jeans and a T-shirt. My jeans, however, are not ball-achingly tight like those of the rest of the men in this place. They're loose and comfortable. No boots for me either. Good old sneakers. I reach up and pat my head. I *am* wearing a hat. No cowboy hat, though. A baseball cap. I take it off and see that it's a blue New York Yankees cap.

Paul. The name Paul flashes in my head. *Who the hell is Paul?*

THE TRACK

Angela pushed back her seat and stood. "Who gave him a New York Yankees hat?"

Robert Stiles clicked a remote, pausing the day's scenario on the array of screens along the wall. A low but audible exhalation of annoyance from the rest of the table.

Stiles turned his attention to Angela, along with the rest of the table. "Is there a problem, Angela?" he asked.

"I wanna know who gave him a Yankees hat," she replied.

"That would be the producer."

"Well, who told him to do that?"

"I imagine he told himself. Are we done?"

"No, we're not. The New York Yankees *mean* something to Calvin. They're his best friend's favorite team. His best friend even *gave* him a Yankees hat. This could jog something in his memory and ruin my pony."

Eleanor Flynn, senior member, another billionaire, leaned forward in her chair. "It's going to take a lot more than a baseball hat to restore your pony's memory, Angela."

"Did you see his face when he looked at that hat?" Angela said.

"I did, yes," Eleanor replied. "Perhaps he was simply momentarily rattled at finding a baseball cap on his head, much as he was rattled to find himself sitting in a clichéd country bar without the first fucking clue as to who he is."

The table laughed.

Angela remained standing, anything but amused.

"Our producers are selected as randomly as the day's cliché, Angela," Stiles said. "They have no background on the pony involved, nor do they care. Their solitary goal is a smooth production. Planting items in an attempt to restore a pony's memory in the middle of a performance would be exceptionally counterproductive to that goal."

Tom Neil joined in. "You ever stop and think that wearing a hat with the word 'Yankees' on it might be the perfect catalyst to start a fight without breaking the rules? The scenario's supposed to be a redneck country bar, for Christ's sake. You say you know the rules; then you should know damn well that hunters can't just sneak up on a pony and cut them down, not if they hope to collect on the job."

"Tom does have a valid point, Angela," Stiles said. "The baseball hat makes a fine catalyst for conflict in our scenario. A wise decision by the producer, if you ask me."

The table nodded in agreement.

Angela forced a smile. "Fine." She took her seat and exhaled. "I'll chalk it up to coincidence, shall I?"

"Please do," Stiles said. "And please recall that my day's bet happens to be riding on your pony as well. If I suspected foul play, I would be just as disappointed as you."

"Fine," Angela said, forcing another smile.

Stiles turned his attention back towards the screen and hit the remote. The day's scenario resumed…

THE SET

"Honestly?" I say to the guy. "I have no idea."

He snorts. "You don't know where you're from?"

"I really don't. To be honest, I don't remember much at all. I'm not even sure how I got here." I chuckle and offer a harmless shrug.

"Hey, Dale," he calls to the bartender. "What's this Yankee faggot's story?"

Okey dokey then.

Adrenaline flushes my belly and swirls hot and tingly. It's a scary, yet familiar feeling. Again, I don't know why. I also don't know why something is telling me that this guy's antics—sitting right smack next to me; calling me a Yankee faggot—is the proverbial

(*I didn't know I knew that word either*)

dog barking before his bite. And that something deep down is telling me not to bark back. To never bark back.

Bite first instead.

Just fucking bite—the fight started the moment this asshole sat right next to me.

The bartender comes over. Wipes his hands on a dirty white towel and then slings it over his shoulder.

"Not a clue," he says to the asshole. "He's cut off though. Wanna show him the door for me?"

Before the asshole can respond, I say, "You mean that door over there?" and actually point *away* from the door, in the wrong direction.

And somehow I know they'll look anyway, the way we instinctively shake hands with someone we don't want to when the gesture is there. Call it societal conditioning, something to do with the limbic brain, or who cares? Point is, they both look where I'm pointing, and I use those few seconds to casually snatch a bottle of Tabasco sauce stacked next to various other condiments on the bar, twist the little red cap, and start to chug it.

Both men face me again, see me chugging the Tabasco, and exchange a funny look.

The bartender laughs. "What the hell?"

The asshole frowns. "The *fuck*?"

I hop off my stool, smile at them both, and then spit a mouthful of Tabasco into the asshole's eyes.

He screams instantly and slaps both palms over his eyes. I kick his stool out from under him, and he drops hard onto his ass yet doesn't seem to care; his whole world right now is the searing pain in his eyes, and he's on his butt and rubbing furiously at them when I pick up his stool and bring it down over his head. *Boom*—goodnight.

I drop the stool and look up just in time to see the bartender reaching behind the bar for something.

I hop over the counter, and he screams. The guy talked tough a minute ago. Now he's about to shit himself. I notice a wooden bat in his hand, the thing he'd been reaching for.

"Whatchu got there?" I ask him.

He actually shows it to me.

"Give it to me and I won't hurt you."

He actually gives it to me. Smiles nervously as if to ask: *Bartender do good?*

I take the bat and ram the butt of it into his solar plexus. He drops to his knees, gasping, and I bring the bat down onto the crown of his head. *Boom*—two sleepyheads now.

I look up, and all eyes in the bar are on me. The music has stopped. A few of the bigger patrons are inching forward. It really is like a frickin' scene out of a movie. I'm waiting for that western whistle you hear before a duel.

"Just a little misunderstanding," I say to the masses with a smile, letting the bat now dangle harmlessly at my side. I plan on talking a blue streak while casually searching behind the bar. The bartender had pulled a bat. Surely there was a gun too. What fucking country bar with a Confederate fucking flag didn't have a gun—or twelve—behind the bar?

This one.

And then, as if that discovery wasn't sobering enough, I notice a far more terrifying one: what fucking country bar with a Confederate fucking flag is full of patrons who *do* have a gun—or twelve—behind their backs?

This one.

At least five patrons are pointing guns at me. One of them is a shotgun that looks capable of splitting me in two.

I drop the bat, raise my hands, and smile again. "Like I said, just a little misunderstanding. I'll be on my way now."

"Come on out from behind there, boy," the guy with the shotgun says, his southern drawl thicker than the asshole's.

Hands still in the air, I slowly make my way out from behind the bar. But first I have to step over the unconscious bartender to do so, and I make it seem as though it's more awkward than it really is, pretending to lose my footing and stumble a little before righting myself. What I'm really doing is using that stumble to drop to a knee and quickly pat the bartender's apron down, hoping beyond hope to find something useful.

I end up finding one of those all-in-one corkscrew/bottle opener thingies that look like a Swiss Army knife and quickly stuff it in my pocket.

I then slowly stand, hands in the air again, and step completely out from behind the bar, towards the exceptionally pissed-off-looking patrons and their armory.

"So how's this gonna go?" I ask. "You're not really gonna shoot me, are you? Over a bar fight?"

The men holding the pistols on me slowly lower them to their sides.

The guy holding the shotgun to my head does no such thing. "You wanna know how it's gonna go, do ya?" he says.

"Yes, please," I say in a condescending tone that seemed to come out on its own.

How the fuck am I this composed? I should be on my knees right now. Oh Christ, maybe soon enough? Nah—these are good old boys. As homophobic as they come. Who would have thought being surrounded by such bigotry would be a relief?

"Smartass Yankee boy," the shotgun says. "This is gonna be fun."

"Can't you guys just kick the shit out of me and toss me in the alley or something?" I say.

Shotgun laughs. "For starters."

Now the bar laughs.

Shotgun waves two guys over. Scratch that; two mountains over. I didn't spot them initially because they were seated. Had they been standing, they would have been impossible to miss.

Man Mountain One takes the lead. He's got the tight jeans, the cowboy hat and boots, the flannel. He's also got a thick black beard, and his lower lip is bulging slightly from chewing tobacco. I know any second now he's going to—*yup!*—he spits a brown glob of chew at my feet. An unspoken challenge, I suppose. A silent bark.

But again, I don't bark; I'm just working out how I'm going to get the first bite in again.

I put my hands in my pockets. "I'm not going to fight you, man," I say.

"Well, I suppose you can just stand there and let him kick the shit out of you, then," Shotgun says, and the bar laughs again.

Man Mountain One finally speaks. "Take your hands out of your pockets and fight like a man, boy," he says.

I shrug and take my hands out of my pockets. In my right fist is the all-in-one corkscrew/ bottle opener thingy. The steel corkscrew attachment is jutting out of the space between my first and middle finger like some kind of medieval weapon. While they were barking, I was flipping the corkscrew attachment open with my thumb.

Time to bite.

In and out like a piston, I repeatedly plunge the corkscrew into Man Mountain One's neck half a zillion times, only stopping when he stumbles back, eyes bulging, frantically gripping his neck with both hands, blood coursing out from between his fingers. He opens his mouth to scream, but only a wet gurgle and a mist of red escape. He drops to his knees, gurgles some more, and then falls flat on his face. A rich circle of blood begins to grow beneath his head.

The place is stone quiet.

I look over at Man Mountain Two. *I didn't sign up for this*, his face seems to say, and he bolts for the exit.

I turn back to Shotgun, panting, corkscrew tight in my bloodied fist, with what I imagine is an exceptionally unstable look on my face.

Who the FUCK am I?

Shotgun slowly lowers the gun to the floor, then stands back up and raises his hands in surrender.

"Okay, that's it. They're all gone. It's over," he says. He then looks over his shoulder towards a wall in back, towards a huge rectangular mirror on the wall. "Is it over?" he says to the mirror.

A disembodied voice, emanating from all around us from some unseen sound system: "Yeah—that last hunter just informed us he's out. I guess that's a wrap, people."

The entire bar takes their eyes off me and starts for the exit, some of them smiling and chatting casually to one another as if the whistle just blew at the factory and it's Miller Time.

The asshole who sat next to me is coming to and starts freaking out about not being able to see. A man and woman dressed like EMTs, carrying their EMT gear, appear out of nowhere and begin tending to him.

The bartender is waking up as well. He too is being attended to by what appear to be EMTs and is prattling on about wanting more money for his injuries; he's an *actor*, not a fucking *hunter*, he says pretentiously.

Man Mountain One? EMTs are helping him as well, but with far less urgency than the asshole and the bartender. After a brief moment, they wave a hand towards the rectangular mirror on the far wall, calling for something. Two guys appear in hazmat suits moment later, carrying a long black body bag.

"Uh…" I say. "Can someone please tell me what the fuck?"

One of the passing patrons pats me on the arm, says, "Good job, man; that was impressive," and then continues to stroll right on past me towards the exit.

Two other patrons walk past me as though I'm not there. "You see the last hunter bail like that?" the one says to the other. "You *know* his handler's pissed. That guy's never working again."

"Kinda can't blame him," the other responds. "Was supposed to be a hackneyed bar fight. Pony turned it into fucking Thunderdome."

They both chuckle and carry on past me towards the exit.

Before long, the entire bar is empty save for me. I'm rooted in the same spot, still breathing heavy, legs rubbery from the adrenaline dump, fist coated in blood and holding a corkscrew that is just as bloody and with what I think might be a chunk or two of fucking *flesh* clinging to it.

"*Hellooo…?*" I call, gaze going all over the empty bar. "Can someone *please* tell me what the hell is going—?"

THE TRACK

"Down he goes," someone at the table said.

They all watched Angela's pony crumble on the spot as if shot from above.

"Waited kinda long to zap him, didn't you?" someone else asked Angela.

Angela slid Calvin's "collar"—a single-button remote the size of a thumb drive—into her breast pocket. "Calvin not's a killer," she said coolly.

"Could have fooled me."

The majority of the table tittered, clearly pleased with the gory compensation for what is typically a deathless cliché.

Angela smiled. "I should clarify. Calvin would make a lousy hunter. He's more like the cornered animal who takes your face off when it's out of options."

"With a fucking corkscrew," another chimed in.

The majority of the table snickered again, the solitary exception Tom Neil. He'd lost his bet with Angela. Worse still, he'd lost a hunter.

Stiles noticed Tom's disgust. "No need to pout down there, Tom. We've all lost a few."

Tom ignored him. Turned to Angela and said: "Your account will be credited by morning."

"You won't forget we doubled down?" she said to him.

"*No*," Tom said through clenched teeth.

"Thank you. Sorry about your hunter. It's a good thing the other one wised up and took off when he did. Calvin can have that effect on people," she said with a sly little smirk, recalling the chaos that ensued following Calvin's Stable implantation weeks earlier.

Tom returned a lipless smile, face reddening. "Yeah—you keep it up, rookie. Next time it won't be some tired old bar fight. We'll see how good your boy is then."

Angela's smirk stayed put. "Yes, we will."

.   .   .

Robert Stiles pulled Angela aside as the rest of the room filed out for the day.

"You made me quite a bit of money today," he said to her.

"Something tells me you're not in this for the money," Angela replied.

Stiles smiled with only his eyes. "Is anyone?"

"Tom Neil didn't seem too happy," she said.

Stiles raised a dismissive hand. "Ah—he's just embarrassed he lost to a first-timer."

"I'd be embarrassed too."

Another faint smile of the eyes. He appeared amused by Angela's frankness. "I don't make it a habit to get background on a pony," he went on. "Unlike an actual racetrack, where background on the horse is paramount, it's all rather superfluous for our…desires, wouldn't you say? As long as everyone gets a good show."

"I suppose. I do enjoy winning though."

"Of course. A good show *and* the thrill of victory."

Angela smiled and said: "So, you were building up to asking me about my pony?"

A proper smile from Stiles this time. A rare sight. *Guilty as charged*, the smile said. "I was, yes. I have high hopes for the boy, especially when things get more…intense."

"As do I."

"I imagine our satellite benefactors were impressed with his performance as well. I expect feedback soon."

"I'm confident," she said.

"And are you equally as confident your boy will be able to handle implantation, should future scenarios demand it?" Stiles asked.

"He's handled The Stable okay thus far."

"Ah, but The Stable has very few triggers that could jog a memory, doesn't it? In their down time, all of our ponies have been programmed to think they're inmates rotting away in a prison cell. Boredom is their biggest threat."

Angela pulled some lip gloss from her purse and dabbed a finger on her lips. "I'm confident my pony can handle anything, implantation or otherwise." She smacked her lips once and put the gloss away.

"And yet you seemed more than a bit rattled earlier when he took considerable note of the Yankee cap on his head."

"It took me quite a while to work my way up to The Track," she said. "Trust would have been an anchor in my journey."

"Trust should be a non-issue at The Track," he replied. "I told you, a good show is all that should matter."

"And I told you I liked to win, and that I trust no one."

A second proper smile. "I must say your candor is a breath of fresh air…and not entirely without merit. In regards to my previous remarks about money being superfluous at The Track, power is anything but. There are many who would like to see themselves in my chair at the head of the table. None of them would ever openly admit this, of course."

"Well, allow me to be the first," Angela said.

Stiles dropped his head and laughed without sound. He held up a slight, bony hand as if to say, *I surrender*. "A *gust* of fresh air," he said.

Angela only smiled back.

"Still," Stiles went on, "as I said, your concerns are not entirely without merit. The lust for power has no ethical leash. Your exceptional success on your first day coupled with your reveling in Tom's defeat may have raised a few pulses at the table."

"I get it," Angela said. "I'm a threat."

"I wouldn't put it as such," he said. "More like a code yellow."

"As long as nobody fucks with my pony, I'm good."

"Such behavior would get them instantly blackballed."

"Only if they got caught."

Stiles frowned a little. "Yes." He pulled a gold cigarette case from his jacket pocket, clicked the case open, and extended it to Angela. Angela declined with an open palm and a polite smile.

Curiously, Stiles did not take a cigarette for himself, merely tucked the case back from where it had come, and said: "Okay—time for some candor of my own, yes?"

"You want to know about my pony," Angela said.

"I do. There's something unusual about him—in his eyes, perhaps—that I can't quite put my finger on. A vulnerability, despite his performance. You said earlier he was not a predator, but more akin to an animal who only kills when cornered. Who was he before all this? Soldier? Cop?"

"Honestly?"

"Please."

"He was a masseuse." Angela winked at him and left.

· · ·

Back home and comfortably retired for the day in her favorite black silk robe, Angela opened a bottle of Dalmore 50-Year-Old whiskey. With only sixty bottles ever produced, Dalmore 50-Year-Old is one of the tastiest and most sought-after whiskeys ever produced. The bottle itself is actually made of a crystal decanter, and the price tag for such a bottle starts at around eleven thousand dollars.

And Angela had zero intention of drinking it.

Not because she couldn't afford it (she could).

Not because she had no taste for scotch, fine or otherwise (she did).

But because this bottle was for Calvin, and Calvin alone. Calvin who loved his scotch and who had sat right here in this very den and enjoyed countless glasses of her finest.

"To think…" Angela said, pouring a glass and setting it next to the enormous flat-screen TV that was replaying the day's scenario of her pony triumphing. "…that I nearly lost you." She dipped two fingers into the glass of scotch and wiped them on the screen. "Enjoy, sexy."

Angela returned to the bar and poured herself a glass of Chateau Lafite Rothschild 2009. She drank slowly and gracefully, the wine briefly staining her full lips that much redder. She glanced at the flat screen once more and recalled how she'd brought Calvin back to life and turned him from a broken ass into a prized pony…

CALVIN'S STABLE IMPLANTATION

WEEKS EARLIER

A knock on Angela's bedroom door.

She stirred and was not courteous in her reply. "*What?*"

"He's watching the tape." A deep male voice on the other side of the door.

She hurried out of bed, threw on a red silk robe, and opened her bedroom door. One of two male assistants she'd employed for the evening was waiting for her. Tall, muscular, deadpan.

"He's been drinking too," the assistant added.

Angela frowned. "What time is it?"

"Noon."

"And he's drinking?"

The assistant nodded. "Started drinking the moment he woke up."

"Silly little lush," she said and nudged the assistant aside to hurry downstairs.

Angela entered the den. Her giant flat screen was on. It displayed multiple squares of camera footage, each square projecting a primary location in Calvin Court's apartment by hidden remote camera. She'd planted these cameras while Calvin was heavily sedated a few nights ago. The center square, the largest, was a direct view of Calvin's sofa in his den, where he sat to watch television. Where he sat now, watching the tape she'd left for him, drink in hand.

The second assistant, also tall, also muscular, also seemingly devoid of affect, sat before the giant flat screen, watching it all, missing nothing, as he'd been instructed to do. He turned upon Angela's arrival.

"He's watching the tape," he said.

"So I heard." She flicked him on the back of the head. "Get up."

The assistant stood and backed away. Angela took his seat, leaned in, and watched with a delight few might ever know. It was one thing to make a puppet dance for you as Calvin had done for her these past several weeks, but it was an entirely different thing altogether to see the puppet completely hollowed out; that precise moment when the puppet learns that nothing had ever been as it seemed. That every string pulled had been to serve ulterior motives even the most cynical of skeptics—of which Calvin was assuredly one—could never fathom.

She'd fucked him good. And the ability to watch his reaction to it now was unequivocally better than any *actual* fucking she'd ever received.

Until he tried to kill himself.

A private hospital setting reserved exclusively for people in Angela's particular line of work and beyond. Calvin Court, stomach recently pumped clean of whiskey and opiates, lay on the operating table, unconscious.

"What about his ear?" Angela asked the doctor.

The doctor pulled the white cotton mask past his chin so Angela might hear him better. "What happened to it?" he asked.

"Someone cut it off. I would think that was obvious."

The doctor pursed his lips in contempt. "The wound looks to have been treated. I see no signs of infection."

"It *was* treated. How soon can you get him a new one?"

The doctor turned towards one of the nurses. "Connie, will you check my desk and see how many ears we have left?"

The nurse stifled a laugh, dropped her head, and looked away.

Angela continued to stare at the doctor, calmly waiting for his answer as though he'd made no such quip.

"His ear will have to be rebuilt with cartilage from other areas of his body," the doctor eventually went on. "Or, if you're in that much of a hurry, we can use a corpse."

"Use a corpse," Angela said. "What about his nose? He told me it would need to be rebroken."

"It will be if you'd like it to be straight."

"I would."

"Okay then," he said. "That should cover most of the superficial damage. The rest will heal with time. Now, why don't we get to the pressing matter at hand, shall we? You wish to make him a pony."

"Yes."

"I was informed that he's a very capable executioner for your film line. Are you sure you want to risk pony surgery? As you well know, I'm the finest surgeon in this industry, and even then, over twenty percent of my patients emerge from the procedure lobotomized."

"He tried to kill himself," Angela said. "I'd say he was done being an executioner, wouldn't you?"

"I suppose. Unless of course you simply see this as an opportunity to play with the big boys." The doctor made no effort to hide the impudence in his tone.

Angela did not give the doctor the satisfaction of volleying his cheek. Composed as ever, she replied: "I've had a standing invite at The Track for some time now. I'm not one to rush into things."

"I see," the doctor said, arrogance still there, but only just in the wake of Angela's calm. "Well, as long as you understand the risks."

"He'll still retain all of his physical abilities?" Angela asked.

The doctor nodded. "He'll be as physically capable as he was before. Full muscle memory."

"And his memory-memory?"

"Wiped clean. Replaced only with The Stable implantation—unless of course he's sent to us for another implantation involving a scenario that demands it."

"What happens to The Stable memory, then?"

The doctor sighed, growing impatient. "Temporarily removed. Replaced with whatever memory is required for the day's scenario. Afterwards—if he survives—The Stable memory will be fully restored, and the prior fully removed. In his mind, it'll be as though he never left The Stable. Would you like me to begin or not?"

"Yes."

"Thank you. The memory and his nose, we can do tonight. He'll have to come back for the ear."

"Fine."

The doctor lifted the cotton mask back over his face and instructed his staff to begin prepping. He looked up at Angela with only his eyes. "You may wait outside," he said.

Angela left.

Angela was on her third cup of coffee when the doctor emerged from the operating room and approached her. The two assistants she'd hired now flanked her like sentries. She had not sent them on their way after kicking down Calvin's door and rushing him here. She was not done with them yet.

"How'd it go?" she asked.

The presence of the two giant assistants clearly unnerved the doctor, and he was uncharacteristically polite this time around.

He removed the white cotton mask covering his nose and mouth, crumpled it into a ball, and put it in his pocket. "Let's just say he's now one of the eighty percent…with a straight nose."

Angela smiled. "Excellent."

The doctor handed her something. A small device the size of a thumb drive. It held a single button.

Angela studied it. "What's this?"

"His collar, if you will. All ponies have one. Call it a failsafe."

"What's it do?"

"Its purpose is twofold," the doctor began. "Like a collar, it keeps your pony in line should he get unruly. It also causes a complete reset, so I would use it judiciously."

"Reset?"

"His memory. It's why I suggest using it prudently. If he's made progress in a scenario, it would be foolish to press his collar. It would start him from scratch again, so to speak. Not to mention render him unconscious for quite a spell."

"And if he *is* being unruly?"

The doctor shrugged. "That's where your judgment comes in. He's your pony now—up to you how to discipline him. My advice? *Let* him run wild. They like unruly. The only time you really want to zap him is when the scenario's over and he's still wreaking havoc. Must draw the line somewhere."

"How long will he be out after I zap him?" she asked.

"Long enough for us to clean him up and get him back to The Stable unaware."

"*Clean him up*—you mean fix any damage he may have incurred during the scenario?" she said.

"Precisely."

"And if the damage is too great to ignore? Broken bones? Stitches? Things that require considerable time to heal? How would that be explained to him when he comes to at The Stable?"

"A minor implantation," the doctor replied.

Angela processed this for a second. "You make him think he incurred it during his stay in prison, in The Stable," she said.

"Precisely."

"When can I see him?" she asked.

"Now, if you like. The nose was a quick fix, and while the memory procedure is quite complicated, the recovery period is remarkably fast. Still, you'll recall that we did have to pump his stomach upon arrival, so he may be rather weak."

"I want to see him."

The doctor handed her a cotton mask. "Might want to wear this."

Angela took the mask but did not put it on. "Why?"

"He knows you well, doesn't he?" the doctor asked.

"Yeah?"

"Well, we don't want to risk jogging his memory, do we?"

Angela looked at the mask again. "Is that common?" she asked. "Something jogging a pony's memory?"

"Not really."

"What's 'not really' mean?"

The doctor sighed, the presence of Angela's assistants beginning to wane in its ability to control his patience. "It means anything's possible. It's unlikely, of course, but why even risk it?"

"Fair enough." Angela put on the cotton mask.

"Wise choice," the doctor said with a patronizing little smile, arrogance nearly back in full swing. "Follow me."

Angela stood by the head of the operating table. Calvin, coming to, blinked up at her. The heavy bruising around both eyes from his broken nose, which had begun healing to a purplish-yellow hue, was now dark and prominent once again from the rebreaking. But it *was* straight. His ear was still absent as ever.

"Hi," she said to him. Her dark eyes shone with benevolence.

"Hi," he replied hoarsely.

"Want some water?" she asked.

"Yes, please."

Angela glanced at one of the nurses nearby. The nurse nodded, left, and returned with a small paper cup of water.

Angela took the cup from the nurse, placed one hand beneath Calvin's head to prop it, then used the other to bring the cup gingerly to Calvin's lips while he took small sips.

Finished, she asked: "Good?"

Calvin nodded and smiled faintly. "Yes, thank you."

Angela handed the paper cup back to the nurse, then slowly lowered Calvin's head back to his pillow. "Do you know where you are?"

Calvin's head rolled from one side of his pillow to the other as he took in his surroundings. He fixed on the nurses, the doctor, and then back on Angela. "Hospital?" he said.

"That's right," Angela replied. "Do you know why?"

His eyes left hers and fixated nowhere, brow furrowed, trying to recall. He blinked and came back to her, lost as ever. "No," he said. "Was I attacked?"

"Attacked in prison, you mean?" she asked.

"Yeah."

Angela glanced up at the doctor. His return gaze was all conceit. The Stable memory had taken.

Angela afforded the doctor a small nod and then brought her attention back to Calvin. "Yes, you were attacked in prison. Nothing serious, though. You're going to be fine."

"I don't remember any of it," he said. "I don't even remember my—"

Angela raised a finger, gesturing for him to be quiet a moment. She then left the operating room and returned moments later with both assistants. One of the nurse's eyes widened at their size. The doctor took a step back.

"*Full* muscle memory too, doctor?" Angela asked him.

The doctor returned a curious frown. "*Yes…?*"

Angela glanced at one of her assistants and nodded.

The assistant stomped forward, snatched Calvin by the scalp with one hand and ripped him off the table, tossing him to the floor.

"*What on Earth?!*" the doctor cried.

"Shut up," Angela told him. She then looked at her assistant and flicked her chin towards Calvin. "Keep going."

The assistant reached down and gripped Calvin by the scalp again, jerking him to his feet. Calvin winced and cried out during the ascent. The assistant flung Calvin into the operating table, knocking it over, instruments falling and clattering to the floor.

Both nurses screamed and rushed out of the operating room. The doctor stayed, too stunned to move.

Calvin, winded on all fours, looked up at his attacker. Then at Angela. "What the fuck *is* this?" he panted out.

The assistant looked at Angela. Angela nodded at him again. The assistant marched towards Calvin.

Still on his knees, Calvin snatched a fallen scalpel from the floor and lunged, cutting deep into the assistant's thigh. The assistant groaned. Calvin jerked the scalpel free and a jet of blood in the face from the assistant's femoral artery was his reward.

Grimacing in agony, the assistant bent and gripped his thigh with both hands.

Calvin did not hesitate; he drove the scalpel upward and into the throat of the wounded assistant—drove it *all* the way in, using the base of his palm to shove in the remainder, the entire scalpel now gone, disappearing into the assistant's neck.

"*Jesus Christ!*" the doctor screamed.

The assistant dropped to his knees, then face-first onto the hospital floor, his femoral artery and neck in a race to see who could bleed the fastest.

Eyes wild and starkly white in a face spackled with blood, his once light blue hospital gown now a patchwork of wet red, Calvin slowly rose to his feet and faced the second assistant—a spot-on visage of an escaped mental patient on a killing spree if there ever was one.

The second assistant turned to Angela, his face sickly pale with fear.

"You can go, if you want," she said to him.

The assistant bolted for the exit, actually hopping over his dying accomplice without a care. The echo of his sprint down the hospital corridor was audible in the operating room until it receded to nothing but the boom of a heavy door being slammed shut in the distance.

"I'll take that as a yes," Angela said.

She faced the doctor. He stood dumbfounded.

"Now what kind of consumer would I be if I didn't test the product before leaving the store?" Angela said to him.

The doctor said nothing.

"Full muscle memory indeed," she said. She then looked at Calvin. "How *you* doing, champ?"

Calvin looked at her and blinked stupidly, mouth hanging open in wonderment, now the mental patient who was coming back to the world, completely unaware of what he'd done or who he was. And why shouldn't he appear as such? Unlike the fleeting visage of the escaped mental patient on a killing spree, this new appearance, the lost patient coming back to the world, unaware of who he was and what he'd done, was more or less apt.

Angela pressed the button on the little remote she'd been given, activating Calvin's collar. Calvin shook once and hard, as if jolted by a strong current, then dropped to the floor, out cold.

Angela removed her cotton mask and grinned. "And the collar works a treat," she said, brandishing it. "You've got one satisfied customer here, doc."

"You're crazy," the doctor said to her in barely a whisper.

"No—I'm a psychopath," she said calmly, holding his gaze. "Just like many of the other people you work for. We are well aware of right and wrong, of what is real and what is not. A man in your line of work should know the difference, doctor."

He actually nodded back at her, as if taking a lesson from teacher.

"I suppose I do have a flair for the dramatic, though," she said. "If I was capable of empathy, I would apologize." She laughed.

The doctor laughed too, a nervous reflex.

"Listen, I'm gonna go," Angela said. "If you could get him back on the table and get that ear fixed, I would really appreciate it. What time is good for you?"

The doctor stammered slightly before replying: "Later this week?"

"Sounds good." She grinned again. "It's exciting, isn't it? I've got a pony!"

The doctor smiled and nodded, another nervous reflex.

"I'll be in touch." Angela turned and left the operating room. Her echoing footfalls down the corridor were light and unhurried. Carefree.

THE STABLE

PRESENT DAY

"Wake up, Twenty-two. Dinner time."

I open my eyes and stare at the ceiling of my prison cell for moment before attempting to get up.

The guard raps my cell bars with his baton. "Let's go."

I sit up and swing my legs over the side of my cot. Rub my eyes and yawn. I stand and approach the cell bars and the guard behind them. He's a big white guy in a beige, short-sleeved button-down with a gold badge over his heart. From the waist down, it's dark slacks with a utility belt that's chockfull of goodies that can hurt and kill.

On his head is a New York Yankees cap.

"Something wrong?" he says to me.

I snap to, suddenly aware that I've been staring at his blue Yankees hat for some reason. "No, I just—your hat."

He tugs the brim. "What? You a Red Sox fan or something?"

Am I? I don't think so. Do I even like baseball?

"No," is all I manage.

He shrugs. "Then what's your problem?"

What *is* my problem? Why do I give a shit about a baseball hat?

It's not just the hat. It's the team.

The Yankees? I don't know anything about them, do I? I'm pretty sure I don't even *like* baseball.

Paul.

The name flashes in my head like a migraine. I shut my eyes tight and press a hand to my head.

"You all right?" the guard asks.

The headache is gone. The memory of the name fading like a dream upon waking.

"Yeah…" I say. "Just a headache." I then consider something. "Is my name Paul?"

He shrugs again. "How the hell should I know? You guys have numbers, not names."

"But I did *have* a name, didn't I? Before I came here? Why can't I remember it?"

"I really don't know, man. Do you want your food or not?"

The memory of the name is nearly gone. Something that starts with a *P*?

"Wait—what was that name I just said?"

"Paul."

"*Right!* Give me a pen."

He gives me a *don't be stupid* face. "I can't give you a *pen*."

"You give us utensils."

He laughs and holds up the cheap plastic Spork they give you with each meal. "Tell you what: If you can break the skin on anyone with this, I'll swap places with you."

"Come on, man, *please*; just give me a pen. I need to write this down before I forget. I'll give it right back."

"Not gonna happen. And your food is leaving in three seconds unless you take it."

I sigh and drop my head. Shuffle over towards the sliding tray carrier to the far right of my cell. The guard places my tray on the carrier and slides it through to me. A diced chicken breast, mashed potatoes, green beans, cornbread, a Styrofoam cup of juice with a lid, and a protein bar for dessert.

A protein bar.

What kind of prison gives you such a hearty meal with additional protein?

"Why so much protein?" I say.

"Huh?"

"Diced chicken *and* a protein bar?"

He frowns at me. "How about you just be grateful?"

Good point. They've got mandatory exercise time here. The protein *does* help. Why mandatory, though, I suddenly wonder. This is America—we revel in our right to be fat.

I ask nothing this time. Just nod a thanks. The guard grunts and leaves.

I take the tray and place it on the little table bolted to the floor right next to my john. Practical design, I suppose.

I take a seat, pick up the cheap plastic Spork, and press the tiny prongs on the end of the spoon into the meat of my forearm. Guard was right; the Spork's about to give, and my flesh isn't even close to being pierced. No way could I do any damage with this thing.

Not that I'd ever have a chance.

I never see any of the other inmates. I can *hear* them shouting from time to time in other cell blocks, but I never see them. Even the mandatory workouts are solitary. Before coming to prison, I'd heard that one of the major problems with prisons is overpopulation, and here I am with my own private cell in my own private block. Made no sense. But then, does any of this? I can't even remember what it was I did to get in here. Can't even remember my own fucking name.

Name.

I *did* remember a name. What was it? Was it mine? Something with a P.

Fuck.

I push back my tray and stand. Head over to the cell bars, lean my forehead against them, and close my eyes.

Something I *can* recall is a constant feeling as though I lived a past life that hasn't completely been erased. Trite as it sounds, snippets come back to me like déjà vu. Transient images that are gone before I can scrutinize them, leaving me with only a feeling of something genuine rather than anything concrete.

The harder I try to recall, the faster the memory seems to fade, but the sensation remains strong, like the way a smell or a song can foster a memory you can feel more than see.

I always chalk this up to things I'd read about

(*when?*)

where the subconscious mind stored stuff away and then gave it back to us without warning, making it seem like new information, when it was just, in fact, old news our brains had processed without telling us, the bastards.

I wonder about reincarnation and past lives and all that. If we *are* reincarnated, where do the memories from our past lives go? Into thin air? Into someone else? Are they like the common lore involving restless spirits in that some of them stick around in limbo until right is made right and they can finally be at rest?

Perhaps I'm the déjà vu in someone else's mind. I am the leftovers in someone else's new life—the parts that weren't completely erased, nothing but fragments of a different time in space, like a periodic role in a schizophrenic's delusions.

Perhaps I simply don't exist.

I pull my head off the bars and stand dumbfounded. Since when did I dig so deep?

Who knows? You don't even know who you are.

True.

Are you drifting again?

Who used to say that to me? *Someone* used to say that to me. I'm sure of it.

Not if you aren't real.

Oh for fuck's sake—I was rambling. Of course I'm real.

I head back to my food and pick up my cup of juice. I pop the lid, take a sip, and instantly choke.

It's whiskey.

Who the hell put whiskey in my juice cup???

I expel the last of the whiskey from my lungs with one final cough and then bring the cup back to my nose. It smells good. Do I like whiskey?

Take a real sip this time and find out.

I do. And I like it.

I take another sip. I like that one too. More so. My stomach burns, but it's a pleasant burn. A familiar one.

Familiar how?

I don't know. Just familiar. Nostalgic, even.

Keep drinking, maybe it'll come back to you.

But when we drink, we tend to forget, don't we?

Some drink to forget, some drink to feel. You strike me as both.

I don't follow.

Forgetting is the result of drinking. It can also be the intention.

And drinking to feel? It seems counterproductive to forgetting. If I want to forget, why would I want to then feel?

Imagine looking out a window at a spring meadow. It's nice, but the window pane blocks you from truly taking it in.

When you drink, you open the window. You can smell the grass, the flowers. Feel the breeze and the sun on your face. God forbid you even get bold enough to actually step through *the window; take a walk in the meadow.*

Okay, I follow. But that's feeling. Where does forgetting fit in?

Say a storm cloud appears on the horizon. Before long it's over the meadow and casting down its darkness. The fury to come.

The sky opens, and the rain falls, powerful and unrelenting, stinging your flesh like a swarm. The meadow is now a terrible place. The sky is black, the flowers are dead, the earth is now a muddy trap that wants to suck you down into a far, far darker place.

I would just leave. I would go back inside.

It's too dark, the rain too disorienting, the pull of the muddy earth at your ankles too strong. You can't just leave. *In much the way someone stricken with cancer cannot just will the disease away, so you too cannot just will the storm away.*

But you can treat it.

You can drink to forget the storm.

True, *the effect is transient, and the rebound effect is sinister, but that is something for Franky Foresight to concern himself with.*

Franky Foresight, the annoying kiss-ass with all his structure and precaution. Man, fuck that guy. We must drink and stay in the moment and feel and keep drinking and forget the storm, bury it deep and bring back the beautiful meadow.

Christ. This insight. Is this me? Has this always been me? How can I stand here and analyze myself so intently when I don't even know who I truly am?

Hell if I know. We are the same person, after all. How about trying more whiskey?

Twist my arm.

I finish the remainder of the cup in a giant gulp and wince from the bite. Everything is getting so much better.

I think someone counted on that.

What?

Someone counted on the whiskey to…I don't know—improve things.

Who counted on that?

I don't know.

Why would they do it? *How* would they do it? Get it inside a *prison*, I mean?

You've heard of loose lips sinking ships? Perhaps whoever it was is hoping for something similar in that vault you call a head. As for how they got it into a prison, your guess is as good as mine.

Loosening my memory with whiskey? Talk about a paradox.

Ah, but we've already established that you're the type who drinks to feel as much as they drink to forget. Perhaps the point is to feel closer to those snippets of your past life. The déjà vus.

That was just philosophical babbling.

Was it? Strange how you can remember very little of your life before prison. Strange how a simple Yankees cap stirs the memory of a name in your head. Strange how someone put whiskey in your juice cup. Strange how you can't even remember your own fucking name.

I get it, it's strange. What do I do?

What can you do? Wait and see if anything new jogs your memory, makes the snippets grow more frequent, last longer. See whether more mystery whiskey arrives and allows you to open the window to the meadow, climb through, and take a walk with nary a cloud in the sky, Franky Foresight having missed his bus, and good riddance.

Am I going crazy? Is this how it starts?

Again, we're the same person. If you're crazy, I'm crazy.
That's reassuring.
I turn back to my tray of food, take a seat, and start eating my dinner.
I wish I had more whiskey.

THE TRACK

WEEKS LATER

They gathered in the elite room in the basement of the mile-high building. Tom Neil was first in attendance. Eager. And why not? Angela's pony was on deck again.

When Angela entered, she could not help but smirk his way. Tom stared back as if she'd kicked his dog. The rest of the members, while civil, were not as polite as they'd been on Angela's first outing with her pony.

Senior-most member Rob Stiles had warned Angela about this. Warned her that some of the members at the track might resent her tremendous first-day winnings, her unavoidable gloating at Tom's expense.

Angela found it counterproductive to focus on such things. Found it far better to focus on the fact that her beloved pony Calvin had sent two imposing men—one of them a hunter—running for the hills after he proved his inclinations to be…*excessive.*

Her pony.

Her pony who'd faced down lethal Russian henchmen in his other life; fed an Australian skyscraper to a giant shark; did every little thing she wanted as long as she kept his dick wet and assured him true affection.

But it would be tougher now. She'd openly betrayed him in his past life, and such hopes of plying his dark mind with promises of incredible sex and genuine affection were no longer realistic. She could only rely on his instincts to be the crazy motherfucker he was—the type who hit first and kept on hitting until the only movements were involuntarily twitches at his feet.

"Not very popular, are you?" Tom whispered to Angela once she took a seat, gesturing to the table as he spoke.

Angela scanned their faces. All of them cold.

"I thought it was all about putting on a good show," she whispered back. "I can't imagine everyone here would be such a poor loser like yourself."

The familiar reddening in Tom's face returned. "You just wait and see what happens today, rookie. Something tells me you won't be so lucky this time."

"Should I take that as a threat? That you fucked with my pony somehow?"

"I don't care how you take it." He then gestured to the table of cold faces again. "Like I said, I'm not the only one here who resents your arrogance."

"Arrogance and confidence are two very different things," Angela said. "I happen to be confident. I'm sorry an insecure beta male such as yourself is so threatened by someone like me."

Tom kicked back his chair and stood. "*Fuck you!* I'm not threatened by you at all!"

"Is there a problem?" Rob Stiles called down from the head of the table.

Angela remained in her seat, inspecting her fingernails with a nonchalant calm, as if nothing had happened. Tom remained standing, huffing, face still red.

"Nothing wrong on my end," Angela said, still inspecting her nails.

"Tom?" Stiles said. "Would you like to sit this one out?"

"No way. With her pony on deck today?" He jabbed a finger at Angela. "*No way.*"

"Then may I suggest you conduct yourself as a gentleman before you're *made* to leave?"

Tom's face reddened that much more. He took a seat.

Angela leaned in to Tom, whispered: "You look like one of those cartoon thermometers that pulses red at the tip just before it blows. You need to relax, Tommy."

"Fuck yourself," he whispered back. "You won the lottery with that stupid bar fight scenario last time. It's the easiest cliché on the wheel. I can't *wait* to see what you get this time."

"Want to double down again? Or don't you have any hunters left? Or any hunters with a decent set of balls, that is?"

Tom's upper lip curled in disgust. "I'll double down once you spin."

"Where's the fun in that?" Angela said. "Why not do it blind? Take a risk?"

He answered through clenched teeth. "Fine."

Even though they'd been whispering, the body language in their exchange might as well have been shouting, at least from Tom's end. Rob Stiles, along with the rest of the table, was anything but blind to it.

"Are you two done down there?" Stiles asked.

"Quite done," Angela said.

"Well, then, as this happens to be your pony's day, Angela, would you mind giving the wheel a spin so we can begin?"

Angela nodded. The remote was handed down the length of the table towards her. She took it, hit the proper button, and the wheel began its spin, hundreds of potential clichéd scenarios flashing on the giant screen before them, too fast for the naked eye to catch at first, then slowing to build tension, then finally trickling to a stop.

Tom was the first to grin.

The remainder of the table oohed.

"Going to be quite a bit different this time, Angela," Stiles said from the head of the table. "We're talking deep implantation on this one. Many hunters involved. Survival rate is low. You, of course, always have the right to pull your pony at the last minute, though it *is* generally frowned upon."

The table nodded and murmured in agreement.

Angela looked at Tom. "Still wanna double down?"

Momentarily flustered by her immovable confidence, Tom quickly gathered himself. "Hell yeah, I do," he said.

Angela looked at every member one by one and then finally fixed her gaze on Stiles seated at the head of the table, his fingers steepled beneath his chin, waiting.

"Let's do it," she said.

THE STABLE

The boom of the steel doors down the corridor stirs me. The series of heavy clanks that are the switches being thrown before light flickers, then explodes into the cell block, and thus my cell—with all the courtesy of a belch in the face—officially wakes me. I shut my eyes tight to the blinding light and pull my blankets up over my head.

It's not time to get up yet, is it?

I hear the increasing clacks of the guard's shoes as he approaches, the clacks eventually stopping outside my cell, a rap of his baton on the iron cell bars seconds after.

"Wakey, wakey, Twenty-two," he says.

I poke my head out from beneath the sheets and squint his way. "What time is it?" I ask.

"It's time to get up. Let's go." Another rap on the bars with his baton.

Something's not right here. There's no clock in my cell, but my body is all the clock I need. Prison time is the very definition of routine and structure. It conditions certain needs and responses to become machine-like over time. When to eat, when to sleep, and when to wake.

My body did not let me know it was time to wake.

I throw back the sheets, swing my legs over the side of the cot, and sit there for a moment, rubbing sleep from my eyes.

I look over at the guard again. "Seriously, man, what time is it? It feels too early."

"I give zero fucks how you feel. Let's go."

I look to either side of the guard. I see no cart carrying my breakfast, and I didn't hear the always-squeaking wheels of the meal cart being pushed, either. When they take you to work out, they make sure you've got a good breakfast in you first. So where are we going?

"Go where?" I ask.

"Big day today, Twenty-two," the guard says to me. "Gotta get you prepped and ready for surgery."

"*Surgery?*" I hop to my feet. "What the hell are you talking about?"

The guard twirls his baton in his right hand, a casual and unconscious movement he's likely done a million times. "Tell me something," he says. "You like horror movies, Twenty-two?"

My confusion must be smeared across my entire face, because he smirks and repeats himself when I don't answer.

"*Do you like horror films?*" he asks again.

I shrug, frowning. "Yeah…I guess. What did you mean by surgery?"

"What's your favorite horror movie?"

He's deflecting my questions, and it's annoying me. "I don't know, man," I say quickly, not even giving it a second's thought. I'm not even sure I've even *seen* a horror movie before. "What did you mean by—?"

"Think you could *survive* one?" he says, still smirking, still casually and unconsciously twirling his baton in his right hand. It's like we're having two entirely different conversations.

"What the hell are you talking about?" I say. "Tell me what you meant when you said I had to get prepped for—"

.   .   .

Angela Thorne soon approached the outside of Calvin's cell, his "collar" in her left hand, thumb still hovering over the single button she'd recently pressed.

Calvin lay fast asleep on his cell floor.

The guard turned towards Angela, looked her up and down with none too much subtlety, his intentions blatant. "So your pony's going to The Track for round two, huh?"

"I abhor rhetorical questions," she said to him.

"Just making small talk, sweetheart."

"I also detest small talk. Men who use pet names for women they just met, more so."

The guard rolled his eyes and adjusted his belt, looking as though he'd have preferred to adjust his crotch so that he might reassure himself in the wake of Angela's gelding.

"Okay, your highness," he began, "shall I make the call for them to come and collect your boy, or is asking for help something you detest as well?"

Angela faced the guard. "Make the call," she said. She then turned back to Calvin and blew him a kiss before leaving. "Knock 'em dead, sexy."

CLICHE
EPISODE TWO

THE SET

He's walking me towards the cluster of cabins where all counselors reside during their summer tenure.

"It's nice to get someone on board who's not easily spooked by legend," he says.

I stop walking. He continues a few more steps before realizing I've stopped, stops himself, and turns. "You okay?" he asks.

"What do you mean by legend?" I ask.

He sighs. "So you *don't* know."

"Know what?"

He sighs again. "I probably shouldn't even tell you, but you'll almost certainly be hearing it from the other counselors soon enough."

This guy—*what the hell is his name again? Gary? George? Greg?*—is starting to annoy me.

"Tell me *what*?" I say.

"This camp," he says. "The legend surrounding it. You really haven't heard?"

"No," I say flatly. "I haven't heard."

"Five years ago? Seven counselors murdered?"

"Dude, *I haven't heard*."

He sighs yet again. "1981. A little over five years ago. Seven counselors were murdered before camp even officially began. One counselor survived. They pinned the murders on him, but he swears it was someone else. Some guy wearing a mask."

"Mask?"

"Yeah."

I give a dry chuckle. "Cliché much?"

Now he chuckles. Except I get the feeling he's not chuckling at my wit. I get the feeling he's chuckling at a joke I'm not in on.

"I miss something?" I ask.

He stifles his chuckle and shakes his head. "No—it's nothing."

He's lying. But fuck him. "So, this guy that survived, the counselor, where is he now?"

"Well, that's the thing," he says. "He was put into a hospital for the criminally insane."

I stop walking again. And again he continues a few feet before realizing I've stopped. Turns and says: "What's wrong?"

"Is this the part where you're going to tell me he escaped?" I say.

He nods. "Matter of fact, I am."

I give an exaggerated roll of the eyes. "I thought you *needed* counselors."

"We do."

"Then why do I feel like you're trying to deter the new guy?" I say. "Your sales pitch needs work."

He shrugs. "Well, like I said; you'd have heard about it from the other counselors sooner or later. Better you hear it from me."

"You also said it was a legend. Why should a legend bother me?"

"Well, the murders *did* happen; that part is true. But then, of course, after…"

"After?"

"During the five-year interim we've been shut down, curiosity has gotten the better of more than a few people. Literally."

"Let me guess again: Legend seekers snuck their way into the camp during that five-year interim, only to never be heard from again."

He studies me for a moment before saying: "That's right."

I roll my eyes deliberately again. "Kind of lacking in originality, isn't it? It's 1986. You just summed up the plot for every slasher film made in the past decade. Your hazing needs work too."

"This isn't hazing," he says. "Not one bit."

"Sure. So then what's the general consensus?" I ask. "Has the counselor who escaped the loony bin returned to the scene of the crime to add more notches onto his knife now that we're open for business again? Or was there really a killer with a mask who still roams the woods, just waiting to slice us all up? Slice us all up after we indulge in premarital sex and drugs, of course."

"Take your pick," he says. "I think either one is somewhat unsettling, don't you?"

"For sure. What kind of mask did the counselor say the boogeyman wore?"

"A ski mask. A black one."

"Cool. If I see anyone wearing a black ski mask, I'll hit first and ask questions later."

He smirks at me, and I get the feeling the smirk holds the same mystery of the chuckle I wasn't in on. "Yeah—I've heard that about you," he says.

I frown his way. "You heard *what* about me?"

He clears his throat, clears away the smirk. Stands upright. Professional head counselor guy again. "Just that you're strong and assertive, is all. We need counselors like that. The summers can get trying, test one's will."

"Especially when there's a dude in a black ski mask going around, fucking people up."

He throws me a disappointed look, as though I'm a kid who just cursed in his classroom. "Please try to get that type of language out of your system before the children arrive."

"Sorry."

We arrive at my cabin. It's a sorry-looking thing. One step above a fort my buddies and I might have built when I was a…

When I was a…

"Nick?" he says to me.

I can't remember my childhood.

"When I was a…" I now mumble aloud.

"When you what?"

It was right there a second ago. It was *right there*. It left the moment I fixed on it, like a rabbit down a hole.

47

(*Down the rabbit hole. How much more apt of an analogy can you make?*)

Who is this? How did you get in my head?

(*Good question. I'm not real sure how I got here myself, or how long I can stay.*)

I drop to my knees. My head starts pounding. I see flashes of blinding light and shut my eyes. This does nothing. Actually seems to make it worse. It's like the hangover to end all hangovers...

(*And you know a lot about those, don't you?*)

Doesn't everyone?

(*Not like you.*)

"Nick??"

What does that mean? What did you mean by "down the rabbit hole"?

(*That lump you call a mind, little bunny. They've dug themselves quite the hole.*)

Who? Who has?

(*Do you even remember getting here?*)

The pain is gone, suddenly and inexplicably. Worse still, I don't even remember—

"Nick???"

I look up at him and blink stupidly, like a man who's just been stirred from a dream, shocked to find the waking world around him. And why not? That's pretty much what just happened, isn't it? I might not remember shit, but I can certainly feel something. Something just happened. Like a seizure or something. Did I just have a seizure? Am I prone to them? I don't think so.

I get to my feet and begin dusting dirt and leaves off the knees of my jeans.

"Jesus, man, are you all right?" he asks me. His concern looks genuine. No, wait—it's not concern. It's shock. His *shock* is genuine. Bordering on fascination, the way a man looks at a lit fuse, both wary of and eager for what it will do.

(*He knows about the rabbit hole.*)

My headache comes back like a blast of white light. I cry out, shut my eyes, and slap both hands onto the sides of my head and—

It's gone again.

Just like that.

I open my eyes and slowly lower my hands from the sides of my head.

"I think you need a doctor," he says. He then repeats, "I think he needs a doctor," into the sky, to God, perhaps. "Something is clearly wrong with his implant, and I don't want to be near him when he blows."

Implant? What the fuck is this guy—?

THE TRACK

Members of The Track watched the day's pony, Calvin Court, drop unconscious before the head counselor, their source of view endless screens of various sizes along all four walls of the room, each depicting, with pristine clarity, any and all sights they needed seeing concerning the day's event.

"*Down he goes!*" Tom Neil said with great pleasure. He spun in his chair towards the far end of the rectangular table where Angela Thorne sat, his grin blinding. "Couldn't even make it to his fucking cabin."

Angela, holding Calvin's "collar" (a small device the size of a thumb drive used to keep ponies in line; one press of its single button and they dropped like rocks), brandished the small bit of technology she'd just pressed as though it was damning evidence in a trial.

"I *had* to leash him!" she fired back. "Who the fuck told the actor to break character?"

Grin as wide as ever, Tom replied: "It's clear your 'badass' little pony couldn't handle the implant." He clucked out a mocking *tsk tsk* sound. "Too bad."

"And that's *my* fault?" Angela said. "I think The Stable has some fucking questions that need answering."

Someone deliberately cleared their throat at the head of the table. Robert Stiles. The senior-most member at The Track. Seventy, exceptionally thin, in a handmade suit from the finest tailors in Italy, wealthier than God.

Both Angela and Tom spun his way.

Stiles hit a master remote, and every screen in the room went black. "Your language is both unnecessary and off-putting," he said to them. "I would like it if we could proceed without your vulgarity *and* hostility towards one another."

There was no love lost between Angela Thorne and Tom Neil. Angela was still a relatively new member at The Track, yet she'd had fabulous success with her pony, Calvin, on her very first day, something Tom Neil resented intensely. That, and finding Angela ridiculously attractive, as did most men, only raised his level of contempt for her. Such beauty and strength from the opposite sex threatened—secretly frightened—the likes of Tom Neil, demoting his behavior to teenage nonsense. Such a threat, if he could not control it, needed to be ridiculed and ostracized in hopes that his peers would catch on and follow suit, reducing the threat to something manageable, to something that no longer appeared on the radar of the Tom Neils of the world.

Except controlling the likes of Angela Thorne was a lesson in futility. Her guile in obtaining her wants was the mosquito to the sharks that were most ego-governed minds—claiming countless more victims by donning the seemingly innocuous wings of the insect as opposed to the screeching siren of the dorsal fin.

Still, she was not immune to frustrations concerning possible foul play. "I apologize for my language," she said to Stiles. "But my concerns stand. Something was wrong with his implant, and it's my opinion that the actor should not have broken character like he did."

Stiles held up a mollifying hand. Arthritic knuckles bulged on his spindly fingers. "Your concern is noted, Miss Thorne. Also not without merit. The actor should *not* have broken character. However, I believe no investigation on the implantation is needed. Likely, it just needed a bit longer to take; perhaps we pushed him too soon into the event before it did."

"So what does that mean?" Angela said. "Will we run it again?"

"*Whoa, whoa, whoa,*" Tom blurted. "No way. She hit his collar; that erases everything." He spun to Angela. "Game over, sweetheart."

Angela swallowed disgust, blinked once, long and slow, then brought her attention back on Stiles as though Tom had said nothing. "Will we run it again?" she repeated. "I hit my pony's collar because the actor broke character. Doesn't that grant me a do-over?"

"*No way,*" Tom blurted again.

Now it was Stiles who held his blink for a spell. When he opened his eyes, they were fixed squarely on Tom. "For the better of your future here at The Track, Mr. Neil, I would suggest you keep quiet until this matter is sorted."

Tom reddened. His lips disappeared. He only nodded his understanding.

"Thank you," Stiles said to him. He brought his attention back on Angela. "We will grant you a 'do-over,' as you call it—"

Tom shifted in his chair, huffed through his nose. Stiles placed a cold eye on him yet continued speaking to Angela without missing a beat.

"—but know that we are granting you this privilege just this once. If you prematurely hit your collar again, for any reason, it will be chalked up as a loss. Are we clear?"

Angela nodded once. "Clear. And thank you."

Stiles gave a single nod back. The rest of the table, minus Tom Neil, of course, seemed just fine with the decision.

"May I say something else?" Angela asked.

Stiles gave a small splay of his hand, inviting her.

"You say the implant was fine, that it just needed longer to take. I disagree. I believe it was faulty. Deliberately so."

The table exchanged curious glances.

"And your evidence is?" Stiles asked.

"I don't have any right now. All I have is a hunch. But I do believe someone is trying to sabotage my pony. To make him remember his former life."

"This is ridicul—" Tom started.

Stiles held up a hand, silencing him like a switch. "A hunch," he said to Angela. "You'll forgive me, Miss Thorne, if I don't—"

"The Yankees cap," Angela continued. "Calvin's first event—in the honkytonk bar—he was given a New York Yankees cap to wear. I explained its significance to all of you that day. In his former life, he cherished a New York Yankees cap that his best friend had given him. I found it a suspicious accessory to outfit him with."

"And, if you recall, we found it to be a *wise* accessory chosen by the producer. A 'Yankee' cap had potential to be a strong catalyst for starting a fight in a redneck country bar. You know rules: Hunters can't just sneak up behind a pony and eliminate them, not if they wish to get paid."

"Those were my *exact* words at the time!" Tom all but screamed.

Stiles hit a different button on the master remote. A guard—black suit, crew cut, white earpiece, barn-door shoulders—entered seconds later.

"Can you please show Mr. Neil out?" Stiles said to the guard. "He's done for the day."

"*What?*"

Stiles would not afford Tom a reply—not even a glance—as the guard began to escort him out.

"So I don't get to participate in the day's cliché?" Tom asked.

Eleanor Flynn, senior member, who obtained her billionaire status by starting multiple foundations for the needy and now passed her time watching and betting on the deaths of innocent men and women for sport, said: "Your bets are already in place, Tom. You'll be notified of the results."

Tom glanced back at Angela. She winked at him. Rage turned his face purple. He left with the guard behind him.

"As we were saying," Stiles continued, "we all agreed that the baseball cap had been a wise—"

"There's something else," Angela said. "Someone gave him whiskey. In his stable."

"I beg your pardon?" Stiles said.

"Someone gave him whiskey. One of the cleaning crew told me. Said when he brought Calvin's tray back to the kitchen, he popped the lid of his juice cup to clean it and recognized the smell instantly. He even dipped his finger into the drop or two that remained and tasted it. It was whiskey. He wanted to know if it was me who had snuck it to him. It was most certainly not."

"How long ago was this?" Eleanor asked.

"Few weeks ago. Not long after his first event."

"And you're just telling us now?" Stiles said.

Angela shrugged. "Point is, Calvin had a drinking problem in his past life. Whiskey was his poison. Maybe you can explain the Yankees cap as a wise decision by the producer, but are you going to tell me that you make a habit of giving ponies booze in their juice cups?"

"No," was all Stiles said.

"So then you understand my…paranoia."

"I assume you want to blame Tom?" Stiles asked.

"Actually, no. Yes, he would have access to the surgeons performing the implantation—perhaps pay them well to sabotage it—but how could he know about Calvin's drinking problem? His preference for whiskey? And if the Yankees cap was *not* a wise call by the producer, but a *deliberate* attempt to jog Calvin's memory, how on Earth could Tom know about Calvin's affinity for that hat too? And, if you'll forgive me for being blunt, Tom strikes me as more cunt than cunning."

A male member in the middle of the table bit back a laugh and looked away. Even Stiles himself looked on the verge of a smirk.

"So, who do you wish to blame?" Eleanor asked.

Angela shrugged again. "I suppose someone whose best interest was to see me fail miserably at The Track. Or, more importantly, to have Calvin regain his memory and exact some kind of vengeance on me. On *us*, perhaps."

The table exchanged curious glances again.

"Given our security measures, that would be quite the trick for a massage therapist," Stiles said.

Now the table chuckled.

Angela stayed composed. "I would have those who underestimated Calvin come in and testify to his capabilities, but they're all, you know…dead."

"Witty, Miss Thorne. Have you considered the possibility that the one who is feeding him whiskey and possibly fitting him with Yankees caps is his dear friend you mention?"

"Given your security measures? That would be quite the trick."

Angela's continued cheek finally brought that smirk to the corner of Stiles's mouth. When his mouth became a straight line again, he gave a genuine nod of respect and said: "The whiskey matter will be looked into."

"And the implant?"

"The same implant as before will be used again."

"Even though it was clearly faulty?"

Stiles sighed. Looked away for a moment, then brought his attention back to Angela. "I'm still not convinced it was, but I'll contact Surgery regardless—have them double-check the existing implant and then add a thing or two."

Angela frowned. "*Add?* Add what?"

"Backstory. The actor wasted enough of our time breaking character, therefore the backstory he went on about at the start will already be implanted into Calvin when we resume—our day's event already in progress, so to speak. Think of it as fast-forwarding through the boring bits and getting to the meat."

The table murmured excitedly to one another.

"What about the actor?" Angela asked. "The head counselor guy? Greg."

"His real name is Anthony," someone said.

"Whatever. Is there any chance Calvin might remember him breaking character?"

"That will soon be irrelevant," Stiles said.

"How so?"

"Call it a lesson. A strong incentive for actors under our employment to never break character. Ever."

THE SET

The flimsy metallic bang of the screen door wakes me with a start, and I sit bolt upright in bed. It's Courtney, another first-year counselor like me, eighteen (not like me), smoking hot, inappropriately dressed in shorts too high and a tee too tight. No bra. She is standing by my cabin door, panting, clearly freaked out. Lightning flashes through my cabin window and the screen door she just burst through. Thunder cracks a moment later. I can hear heavy rain pelting the roof. Wind is making the flimsy screen door rattle.

How long have I been asleep?

"Courtney?" I say. "You all right?"

"I think…I think I need help," she says, voice trembling.

I hurry off my bed and approach her. "What do you mean? What's wrong?"

"I'm not really sure. But Lynn's bed…"

"What about it?"

"It's covered in blood."

Say *whaaat*?

"What the hell are you talking about?"

She looks like she's about to cry. "It's like I said—her bed is literally *soaked* in blood."

Soaked.

Soaked…

Soaked?

Why isn't *she* soaked? Her hair's not wet. Her clothes are dry (shamefully, this girl in a wet tee-shirt would have been the *first* thing I noticed). Lynn's cabin is at least a hundred yards away.

"Why aren't you wet?" I ask.

Her frightened face is now a quizzical one. Almost as if my question has made her completely forget what she just professed to have seen.

"Huh?" she says.

"You just came from Lynn's?"

"Yeah…"

I gesture towards her

(*boobs*)

tee-shirt. I gesture towards her hair. "Your clothes are dry. Your hair is dry." I look past her through the screen door, out into the rainy night, then back on her. "How the hell did you get here from Lynn's cabin without getting wet?"

She gapes at me for a moment. Then: "What the hell is wrong with you? I just told you Lynn's bed is soaked with blood, and you want to know why I'm not wet?"

"That's right. I'm not a fan of practical jokes at my expense."

"This is no fucking joke, asshole. I'm telling you the God's honest—"

The screen door is jerked open. Greg, the head counselor, steps inside, looking frantic. Now *he's* soaking wet, and yet…*he's holding an umbrella?* What the actual fuck?

"What the hell is going on?" Greg asks. "Where the hell *is* everybody? I can't find a soul."

"I have no idea," Courtney answers.

"I heard screaming," Greg says.

"That was me," Courtney says. "I went to Lynn's cabin and…"

"And what?"

"She wasn't there, but her bed was…it was soaked in blood."

Soaked.

Greg's eyes widen. He goes to speak, but I cut him off.

"You've got an umbrella," I say, motioning to the umbrella dangling in his right hand.

He looks down at it, then back up at me. He's wearing the same quizzical face that Courtney was. The one that seems to instantaneously make you forget about the prospect of bloody beds.

"Yeah? *So?*" he says.

I wave a hand up and down his dripping body. "Well, you clearly didn't use it. Why?"

"It was outside your cabin door. I brought it in with me." He frowns hard. "What the hell is wrong with you?" He hands the umbrella to Courtney. "I'm assuming this is yours?" he says, gesturing to her dry status.

She takes it from him. "Thank you." She spins back towards me. "*Happy?* Is your little mystery solved?"

"As to why you're dry? Sure. As to why there's blood on Lynn's bed? No."

"You don't think…?" She turns to Greg, her freaked-out status seemingly climbing that much higher.

"Oh, come on, Courtney, I told you; it's a legend," he replies. "You were clearly creeped out by it at orientation, and I'm sure everyone took note. My guess is that this is all a prank. Everyone missing…the blood on Lynn's bed…all a prank."

"You didn't seem too convinced it was a prank when you burst in here," I say to him.

"It *has* to be. There's simply no way—"

The screen door is jerked open yet again. In steps a big fucker wearing a black ski mask. Gripped tight in his right hand is a machete.

I quickly shuffle back towards my bed.

Courtney screams and backs up with me.

Greg screams yet stays rooted on the spot.

The big fucker takes Greg's head clean off with one swipe of the machete, the head hitting the ground and rolling unevenly towards Courtney's feet. The eyes on Greg's severed head are open; one of the lids flutters rapidly. His headless body drops to its knees, then falls forward. Blood comes out of the stump like a busted hydrant. His legs and arms convulse.

Courtney stops screaming. She stares down at the body in disbelief.

Except her face is all wrong.

It's the wrong *kind* of disbelief. I've seen it before. It's the same quizzical look both she and Greg wore minutes ago. The look that doesn't fit the circumstances.

"How can that be fake?" she mutters to Greg's corpse. Then, curiously, to the killer, and with more oomph: *"How can that be fake?"*

It's clearly too surreal for her to process. She's probably clinging to Greg's whole practical-joke theory.

I, however, am fucking *not*. I make a mad dash for my cabin window.

Courtney stays put, disbelieving gaze ping-ponging between Greg's corpse and the psycho who lopped his head off.

"How can that be fake?" she asks the psycho again.

Both Greg and Courtney asked what the hell was wrong with me just moments ago. Now it's my turn.

"What the hell is wrong with you?!" I've got the window open. The storm is raging now. Rain sprays my face. *"Get over here!"*

The masked killer just stands in the doorway, chest heaving, bloody machete gripped tight at his side.

Being frozen with fear and disbelief, I can understand. But actually *approaching* a big dude in a mask who just chopped a guy's fucking head off in front of you as though you mean to reason with him? Insane.

Yet it's exactly what Courtney is doing, but not before she nudges Greg's severed head with her toe

(*???!!!*)

with the uncertain face of someone kicking over a rock to see whether some creepy-crawly is lurking beneath. The severed head acts as severed heads do, lolling to one side before righting itself again, lifeless and unattached as ever.

She's close to the psycho now. Asks him: "That was fake, right?" She turns and drops her gaze to Greg's headless torso. Nudges *that* with her toe. "Anthony?" she says.

Anthony???

Her back to the killer, she does not see him slowly raise his machete overhead. I do, though, and I scream her name.

Unfortunately, all this does is make her look at me, her face no longer the quizzical, doesn't-belong-under-the-circumstances face, but more a face of one being disturbed from a private conversation, borderline annoyed to be interrupted. Natural selection at work, perhaps; maybe the idiot *should* die.

Ah shit, that's a bit harsh. I should—*Whoop!* Too late. She's dead.

Courtney drops hard to the cabin floor, machete buried in her skull, her limbs convulsing just as Greg's had.

The killer yanks the machete from Courtney's head and turns towards me. His stance is as it was by the cabin door: chest heaving, bloody machete gripped tight to his side, black holes in that ski mask staring at me.

I have no intention of staring back. I leap through the window and haul ass.

THE TRACK

MOMENTS BEFORE...

The table watched the "remastered" edition of the day's event unfold on the walls of monitors with a collective look of concern, the reason both Calvin's astute eye and the director's lack of one.

Calvin: "Your clothes are dry. Your hair is dry. How the hell did you get here from Lynn's cabin without getting wet?"

"*Goddammit*," Stiles muttered, pulling out his phone. The director answered on the first ring. "Are you seeing this?" Stiles scolded. "How could you fucking miss something like that? Get Anthony in there with an umbrella *now*. Tell him to say he found it outside the cabin; it was Gillian's; that's why she's not wet. Make sure *he's* wet, though."

The table soon breathed a collective sigh of relief when Anthony appeared and performed as he was told.

Stiles pulled his phone again. "Go ahead as planned with Anthony," he said to the director.

To the table's great delight, the monitors soon showed Anthony's beheading.

Angela could not hide her surprise. "*Jesus*—was that real?"

Stiles smiled her way with only his eyes. "Incentive to never break character."

And then Gillian apparently shared Angela's skepticism, and the table was concerned once again.

Gillian AKA Courtney: "How can that be fake? *How can that be fake?*"

Stiles pulled his phone yet again. "*Are you fucking kidding me?*" A brief pause as he listened to the director. "*Of course!*" He hung up.

Back to the monitors.

Calvin: "*What the hell is wrong with you?! Get over here!*"
Gillian: "That was fake, right? Anthony…?"

Stiles threw up his hands. "Oh, for the love of *God!*"

The hunter brought the machete down onto the top of Gillian's head, killing her instantly. The table exhaled both relief and delight.

After Calvin fled through the window, Stiles snatched his phone from the table (considering how the day had been unfolding, he knew better than to tuck it away again) and phoned the director for the fourth time. The previous record for necessary calls to a director had been two, and that was when The Track was just finding its feet. Many a fan would be battered with shit before the day was out.

"Get in there and clean them up quickly. Do not—do *not*—alert the other actors to their demise. If they know, their performance will be shaky for the remainder, no matter how much money we throw at them. What? We'll tell them when it's over, won't we? Those who want to stay can stay. Those who want to go…" He needn't finish. It was well-known that if there was anything Stiles abhorred more than incompetence, it was loose ends. "And turn off the goddamn storm already; he'll have to swim to the next scene if you keep it going so strong."

Stiles hung up. His usual stoic demeanor came over him again like a trance. He did not bother to address the table as to the specific goings-on behind the scenes; they'd heard the conversation. He merely turned his attention back to the walls of monitors, as did the rest of The Track, and resumed watching Calvin's attempt at escape.

THE SET

The storm breaks (breaks instantaneously, in fact), and I'm now slogging my way through a muddy path until I reach Greg's head counselor quarters, although I suppose now he's no longer "equipped" to hold that title.

I go inside, and blood is everywhere. And I mean *everywhere*. On the walls, the floors, the furniture, the *ceiling*. It all looks so…

(*Deliberate?*)

Of course it's deliberate. They're all dead. The fucking psycho painted the room with their blood.

(*If they're all dead, where are they? And why waste time painting the room with their blood when there's me, Courtney, and Greg to kill? Why do it all? It's too excessive. It serves no purpose.*)

Since when does sound reasoning factor into why a homicidal maniac does what he does?

(*When said maniac is doing not what he does, but what he's told.*)

Huh?

An ear-splitting screech scares the shit out of me and spins me like a top.

It's Carly, another counselor, standing in the doorway, looking around the bloodied room in wide-eyed disbelief. Carly's nineteen, I think. Sexy as hell like Courtney was. Dressed inappropriately like Courtney was. Shorts too high, tee too tight, no bra. Come to think of it, I'm pretty sure *all* the female counselors are dressed like this. All of them young and hot. Like, inexplicably hot. The men too. All of them ripped young studs showing off their abs and guns. With perhaps the exception of Greg, I'm probably the oldest guy here. Scratch that—I am now officially the oldest guy here.

Why was I hired? Greg was head counselor; he's allowed to be the skinny, dorky older guy. I'm a newbie. I'm fucking up the *Baywatch* bell curve here.

(Baywatch? *What's that?*)

It's a TV show, isn't it?

(*Is it?*)

A sudden flash of light blinds me and sets my brains on fire. I drop to my knees and grip my head in agony. Like a reel on a projector moving at top speed, images flash through my head too fast to grab any one.

Carly runs over to me and drops to her knees, placing a hand on my shoulder. "*Are you okay?*"

I turn my head towards her voice yet keep my eyes shut tight, even though the act holds no sense; the blinding light is coming from *inside* my head, not from anything in the room.

Carly shakes my shoulder. "*Are you all right?*" she asks again.

"*Baywatch*," I say for some reason.

"What?"

I open my eyes and look at her. I see an expression that is becoming all too familiar to me: the quizzical face that doesn't fit the situation.

"What?" I say back.

"What did you just say?" she asks me.

I…can't remember. Christ, it was there a second ago.

A sudden blast of a buxom blonde in a red bathing suit running in slow motion on the beach. I can actually *hear* cheesy music matching her strides. The image scorches my eyes; the music stabs my eardrums. I shut my eyes tight again, and the reel on the projector resumes its dizzying speed, blurring away the once-distinct images of…

(*Of…?*)

I don't know.

"I don't know," I say to her. I then open my eyes, look into hers, and reiterate: "I don't know what I said."

Her face changes back to

(*relief? was that relief I saw first?*)

fear. She helps me to my feet.

"What the hell *happened* here?" she asks. "Where *is* everyone?"

"Greg and Courtney are dead," I say. "Some freak—"

(*freak?*)

"—in a mask—"

(*in a mask? Freak in a mask? You've been here before.*)

Another flash of light. I shut my eyes and grip my head. "*Fuck!*"

"*What?!*" she cries. "*What's wrong with you?*"

I shake away the pain and get to my feet, hesitating a moment before opening my eyes again. The flashes of light are gone. The pain is gone.

"Forget it," I say. "I'm fine." I take her by the hand. "Come on, we need to get the hell out of here."

She jerks her arm free. "*No!* We have to look for the others!"

"Did you hear me? Greg and Courtney are *dead*. I saw them murdered with my own eyes. We need to get the fuck out of here and find some help."

She backs away from me. "We need to help the others!"

What the fuck is wrong with this girl?

The door to Greg's quarters suddenly bursts open, and guess who is in the doorway, same as before: black ski mask, chest heaving, bloody machete gripped tight at his side.

Another ear-splitting screech from Carly is like his starting pistol; he rushes towards me, machete raised. I turn and run towards a coffee table, hop it, then spin and flip it over, creating a barrier between him and me. He snatches the overturned table with one hand, violently tosses it aside, and raises the machete again.

Except his momentary task with the table forced him to reset his attack.

Me? I'm cocked and loaded and punt his nuts up into his throat. He groans and doubles over, and I angle off and kick a second field goal into his face. A good kick too. Like some kind of fucking kung-fu shit. How the hell did I know how to do that? Or who fucking cares? Dude dropped like he was dead, and I couldn't be happier.

I quickly bend, snatch the machete from his unconscious hand, raise it overhead to bury the thing into his skull just as he did to poor Courtney, and… *Carly shoves me away???*

I regain my balance and gape at her. "*What the fuck are you doing?!*"

"We need to go!"

I gesture down with the machete towards the sleeping psycho. "We *need* to finish the fucker off!"

"Leave him! We have to go and find the others!"

"Are you fucking nuts? This might be *the* single greatest fucking cliché in horror films! They never finish the fucker off when he's hurt!"

She ignores me and starts towards the door. "*Come on!*"

*Jesus H…*if the son of a bitch wakes up and catches up to us, I'm gonna let him kill her. More natural selection at work. I'd be doing the world a favor.

I hurry after her out the cabin door, and we head towards a circle of cabins in the distance. An enormous oak is soon the only thing between us and the first cabin, yet the moment we're close, our buddy hops out from behind it and stops our run on a dime.

Impossible. Absolutely, utterly impossible. Can the fucking guy teleport???

Carly screams.

I face her. "*I told you we should have finished him off!*"

I turn back to the killer. He's now wielding an axe. So the guy not only woke up, beat us here, but also had time to snag an axe first? Okay.

(*Who cares? Kill the fucker now. No more running.*)

Amen.

I grip the machete tight in my right hand and slowly raise it out in front.

"*No!*" Carly screams. "*He'll kill you!*"

"Get to the cars," I call back to her, keeping my eyes on him. "Don't stop driving until you find help." I place my full attention back on him. "So, who are you, man?" I ask. "You the counselor who escaped the loony bin? Or are you the *real* killer he claimed was responsible for it all?"

He slowly cocks his head to one side and studies me.

"Why don't you take off your pussy little mask so we can get a look at you."

His chest continues its trademark heaving, quicker and more pronounced now with agitated breaths. He grips the axe tight with both hands.

"Come on, man," I continue, "take off your mask. Let's get a look at you. No, wait—let me guess; you're deformed or something, right? Self-conscious? Face is all jacked up and ugly as hell? Gotta be. This whole night has been one giant hemorrhoid of a cliché. It's gotta be. Come on, take it off."

He grips the axe tighter. His agitated breaths quicken further.

I start towards him. "Fine—I'll take it off myself."

Carly suddenly bolts past us.

She bolts, not for the cars—no, that would have been logical. She instead bolts towards every masked lunatic's preferred stomping grounds since the dawn of masked lunatics. She bolts towards the woods. The deep…dark…desolate…woods. Of course she does.

"*Carly!*" I yell.

She doesn't answer, just keeps running.

If the son of a bitch kills me, he'll assuredly end up killing her too. Can I live with that?

(*You'll be dead, stupid.*)

"*Carly!*" I yell again.

Her fleeing figure is moments away from being swallowed up by the black of the forest beyond.

"*Goddammit!*"

I take off after her.

The killer just stands there and watches me sprint past him. And why not? Fucker will probably materialize out of nowhere some fifty yards ahead.

I hit the perimeter of the forest. I can just make out Carly in the distance, ducking and dodging trees.

"Carly, stop!" I yell. "*STOP!*"

Miraculously, she does, turning and facing me, moonlight shining down on her face almost deliberately so I can see her terror. She's panting like someone who just crossed the finish line.

I catch up to her. "Where the hell do you think you're going?"

"Away from *him!*" she cries.

I hold up a hand. "Okay, just relax, all right? Relax. He didn't follow me."

A body drops from the trees above, landing mere inches from us. It's a man. He's soaked in blood. He looks very dead.

Carly screams.

I look up, hoping the moonlight will give me a glimpse of someone else in the trees. Because there *has* to be someone else in the trees above, right? No *way* did this dead body just happen to fall at the *precise fucking moment* that Carly and I were beneath it. No way.

Only it did. The moonlight is kind and bright; I see nothing in the trees.

Carly screams again, and I know what she's screaming about before I even look.

Yep. There he is. Maybe ten feet *ahead* of us in the distance. Same stance. Same heaving chest. Axe gripped tight in both hands.

Carly bolts again. And I go after her again. She's heading east towards a particularly dense thicket of woods. I risk a quick peek behind us while in full stride and notice that he's following this time. Not running, though, of course. Running would be too un-killer-like. No, our guy is *walking* after us. Although, to be fair, it is more of a power-walking stride, but still walking nonetheless. I suppose if I had as many shortcuts as he did, I wouldn't waste the cardio either.

(*Except you don't believe that, right? Shortcuts? Bodies falling just so. Courtney's and Greg's odd behavior at inappropriate times? Carly's too. Courtney calling Greg "Anthony," for Christ's sake?*)

I keep running towards Carly.

So what does it all mean?

(*You're in a fucking horror movie.*)

Sure—that makes a lot of sense.

(*Didn't say it made sense, but you are. How else do you explain it?*)

Better than that.

(*Any second now, one of four things is going to happen. No—scratch that. All four of these things* will *happen. First, Carly will trip and fall while run—WHOOP!—there she goes!*)

Carly trips and falls hard up ahead. She writhes on the ground, clutching her ankle. I continue after her and risk another peek back

(*you won't see him*)

at the killer. I don't see him.

(Because he's already waiting somewhere up ahead. That's number two. Number three, you'll help Carly up, and a second body will drop from above, right smack next to you guys. Almost as if it were very much alive, perched and waiting to pounce on you.)

I arrive at Carly and bend to help her up. "Are you all right?"

She's hopping on one foot, grimacing in pain. "My ankle...I think it's broken."

I wrap her arm around my neck and shoulder, and we continue on, me her crutches.

"*There's a light up ahead!*" she yells and points.

I look where she's pointing. I can see a faint glow in the distance. A few yards farther, and I can just make out the faint silhouette of a solitary cabin, the glow coming from candlelight in one of its windows.

(Aaaannd...that would be number four. That's where our buddy lives, so to speak. And a hundred to one, whichever bodies aren't dropping out of the sky are almost assuredly stacked in there.)

Well, your number two and number three things haven't happened yet, so—

Another body drops from above, landing at our feet, stopping and sending us back a step like a shove.

Carly screams again.

And then not even a second later, screams *again*...because the killer steps out from behind a tree up ahead.

(*You were saying?*)

"SERIOUSLY?!" I yell to the killer, to the woods, to the colossally fucked-up universe I seem to be trapped in.

(*Might as well dodge him and keep on heading towards that cabin. Shit's gonna play out whether you want it to or not.*)

What if I don't?

(*Don't what?*)

What if I don't want it to play out?

(*Well, then I would do something similar to what you intended to do in Greg's cabin before Carly, yes,* Carly *stopped you.*)

What's that supposed to mean? Carly "stopped" me?

(*Would be a boring movie if the killer was offed so soon.*)

Boring movie for who?

(*For whoever's watching.*)
Watching?
Watching.
Watching…
watchingwatchingwatchingwatchingwatchingwatching—
The bright light is back. The agony in my brain is back.

I drop to my knees. Eventually open my eyes. Carly is staring at me. And—wait for it—she's staring at me with the all-too-familiar quizzical face that doesn't fit the scenario.

I look over at the killer. My vision is a narrowing tunnel. The killer only stares back. I'm a *prime* fucking target right now. Helpless as a bound baby. Why doesn't he attack?

(*Such an easy kill would make for a boring scene. Not very "sporting."*)

I'm gonna pass out.

THE TRACK

Angela kicked back her chair and stood. "Something is *clearly* wrong with his implant!"

"Miss Thorne, please sit down," Stiles said.

Angela remained standing, gestured towards one of the bigger monitors. "That was what? His *third* episode? And now he's out cold!"

"Miss Thorne…" Stiles spoke to her with the disciplined calm of a veteran teacher to a defiant student.

"*What?*"

"Have you considered the fact that your pony's *will* is causing these episodes?"

Angela paused, face scrunched in thought. When it came unscrunched, she said, a bit calmer now: "I thought that was impossible. You all said that was impossible."

"Rare, but not impossible."

"So, what does that mean?" she asked. "Do we start over *again*?"

"Oh no," Stiles said firmly. "No, we are far too deep into the event to start over. They're nearly upon the killer's cabin. The final act."

"Have you been watching him, though?" Angela asked. "Watching him *close*? It's like he's figuring it all out."

"And?" Eleanor Flynn said. "He can figure it out all he wants. If he survives, his memory of the event will be erased before he's returned to The Stable." She splayed a hand. "Standard protocol."

"Quite right," Stiles added. "I would actually be pleased, if I were you, Miss Thorne. Your pony, despite any troubles with his implant you continue to claim he has, dispatched that first hunter most impressively."

"Actually, no he didn't," Angela said. "He was *about* to, but Carly pulled him away. What the hell was that about? Are actors allowed to save hunters' lives?"

"I don't believe the actor was trying to save his life as much as she was trying to keep the cliché running smoothly. Your pony actually said it best: In horror films, they never finish off the killer when they have him momentarily incapacitated. Carly was simply trying to keep that particular cliché alive and well so that the killer could reappear moments later. Which, of course, he did."

Angela shook her head, annoyed. "Call it whatever you want, but my pony had a chance to eliminate a hunter, and your actor saved that hunter. You decreased my pony's odds of survival just as he was seconds away from *increasing* them."

A male member from the middle of the table held up his smartphone and said: "I was just informed that the hunter Miss Thorne's pony kicked has a severe concussion and is in medical care as we speak. He is officially out of the event."

Stiles looked at Angela and offered a polite, if not slightly condescending, little smile. "There, you see? Your pony did eliminate him after all."

"Call me a stickler for certainty, but I would have rather seen Calvin bury that machete into his head."

The table murmured in macabre agreement.

"Be that as it may," Stiles said, "the actor made a judgment call, and we must stand by it."

Angela snorted. "You've had two actors break character so far. And Carly has looked like she's been moments away more than a few times herself."

Stiles sighed. "Your point to all this, Miss Thorne?"

Angela looked away for a moment, searching for the right words. Finally: "Something stinks."

The table murmured disapproval this time.

Angela went on before Stiles could respond. "I'll keep on saying it until I'm blue in the face: Something is wrong with Calvin's implant. Maybe it's his will surfacing—quite frankly, it wouldn't surprise me; it *is* why he's my pony, after all—but I believe there's something else. You can continue to call me paranoid all you want, but...I don't know, something's not right. *Someone* wants him to remember his former life. I don't know who, how, or why, but my hunches have always gotten me very far in life, and I'm not about to turn my back on them now."

Stiles leaned back in his chair and sighed. "I will present you with two options, Miss Thorne. You may pull your pony now from the day's event, and both you and he will never be welcomed back at The Track, with your very strong assurance that you will never mention your time here for as long as you breathe..."

"Subtle," Angela said.

Stiles ignored her understanding of his threat. "...or, you may continue with the day's event as is. Hope your pony wins the day, and hope that his next implant isn't quite as intense. You were warned this particular implantation was quite involved. You were given the option of refusal."

"At my second go at The Track? Yeah, that would have gone over swimmingly."

Stiles gave his patented long blink. "What is your decision, Miss Thorne?"

"Hmmm...life or death? It's a toughie."

"Remember your place, Miss Thorne," Eleanor Flynn warned. "I for one think Robert is being *too* generous in his offer."

Angela flashed a big old phony smile for the table. "*Action*," she said.

THE SET

I wake up facedown. Woodsy debris is stuck to one side of my face. My head aches like a wicked hangover.

Clearly I passed out in the woods.

Was I drunk? My head *does* ache like a killer hangover. Why would I be drinking in the middle of the woods at night? Makes no sense.

I get to my feet and wipe more debris off my clothes. Bits and pieces are starting to trickle back, and then, like a film in a dark theater bursting to life on the big screen, it all comes back at once—as do quite a number of questions.

Carly. Where is she?

(*He took her to his cabin in the distance, no doubt.*)

I spot the dim lights of the cabin in the distance.

Who says it's his?

(*I do. It'll be a sorry-looking thing. Bodies stacked in there. Carly will be tied up, curiously left alive, both of them waiting for your arrival. Such odd behavior for a mindless killer, no? Logic would suggest he'd kill her the first chance he gets. But then logic doesn't apply here, does it?*)

Why didn't he kill me while I was unconscious?

(*Similar to the reason I'd bet our left nut Carly's still alive and waiting for you in the cabin. It would have ruined the ending if he'd killed you while you lay helpless.*)

The bodies. The bodies that fell out of the trees almost on cue. One of them dropped in front of us right before I passed out.

I scan the ground. No body.

Where the hell did it go?

(*Maybe he took it with him to stack with the others in the cabin.*)

Along with Carly? Cumbersome task.

(*True. Unless Carly and the body went on their own accord.*)

That makes a lot of sense.

(*You're hoping to find sense in all this?*)

I start towards the cabin.

(*Pick up the machete first.*)

I stop and look down. The machete is there. He didn't take it with him.

(*Of course he didn't. You starting to get it now?*)

You said sense doesn't apply.

(*For* why *this is happening? No. For what's* going to *happen? Slasher Film 101 shit, man.*)

I pick up the machete and continue towards the cabin.

(*So, what are you going to do? Just walk on through the front door like you're supposed to?*)

I'm open to suggestions.

(*You wanted to finish the killer off when you had the chance, but Carly stopped you. That was wise on your part—going off script. Stay off script.*)

Does it matter, though? The guy is everywhere at once.

(*Is he? There's an old magic trick called The Teleported Man. Do you believe in magic?*)

No.

(*But you know the trick. How was it done? How can one man be in two places at once?*)

It was an old trick done up on stage, the audience pushed well back. Spotlights positioned just so to affect the vision. Misdirects in abundance.

(*Why?*)

My mouth drops open slightly as everything starts to gel.

So they wouldn't notice the flaws in the body double that reappeared after seemingly vanishing into thin air.

(*And how does* our *guy get away with it?*)

He wears a mask.

(*Boom.*)

THE TRACK

The table whispered to one another, their faces collectively puzzled.

It was Eleanor who said: "What's he doing? Is he *leaving*?"

The walls of monitors projected what seemed to be just that: Calvin had done an about-face and now started a casual stroll *away* from the isolated cabin. He even appeared to be whistling a tune as he did so.

"Looks that way," Stiles said.

Eleanor again: "Why would he leave? He must suspect that the girl's inside, that the killer has her."

Angela smirked. "Maybe that's *why* he's leaving."

Stiles cocked his head, studied Angela for a moment. "Help me understand that logic, Miss Thorne."

"Why not wait and see? If I'm right, I'd hate to ruin the surprise." Her confidence oozed.

The slightest twinkle was in Stiles's eye as he stared back. Calvin had made him a significant amount of money in his debut weeks ago. And unbeknownst to the rest of the table, Stiles had placed a substantial amount of money on Calvin to prevail again today, despite the cliché's high difficulty level.

"Fair enough," he said. "Let's see how it plays out, shall we?" Stiles raised the remote and addressed the table. "Anyone object to a bit more volume for the final act?"

The table's eyes never left the screens when they shook their heads and muttered "no."

Stiles turned up the volume. The Track settled in for the final act, none with a more eager eye than Angela Thorne…

THE SET

I continue my stroll through the woods, away from the cabin, whistling louder—intentionally so—than before.

Here fishy, fishy...

I'm halfway back to camp when he steps out from behind a tree, blocking my path. Once again, he wields a machete. No axe.

I gesture to his machete with my own. "How's it going, man? Back to a machete, huh? What, was there only one axe to go around between you guys? Kind of a low-budget production, if you ask me."

His menacing, look-how-scary-I-am stance shifts a little. It's subtle, but I notice.

I begin to inch forward, my encroachment hid behind calm and perplexing speak. Off-script speak.

"How many of there are you?" I ask. "Two? Please say two. It would be so nice if I only had to deal with one other asshole after I kill you."

He lowers his machete and actually says: "*Huh?*"

I use his momentary befuddlement to my advantage and swing with everything I've got, keen on giving him the Greg Treatment. Problem is, Greg was a scrawny dude with a neck as thick as my forearm. Probably felt like cutting through butter.

Not this guy. Neck like a linebacker, the big fucker. The machete gets stuck halfway, robbing me of a clean lop,

(clean lop—*there's something you don't say every day*)

yet the guy crumbles all the same, gurgling audibly beneath his mask for a few seconds before he stops moving.

I bend to remove the mask. Will he spring to life the moment I get close?

(*If he does, then we've been way,* way *off about everything thus far.*)

I pull off the mask. He doesn't spring to life. It's all pretty anticlimactic, actually. Just a guy I've never seen before, looking up at me with dead eyes.

"Meh," I say aloud.

(*What did you expect?*)

I shrug to myself.

(*You wanted the final girl by your side to confirm the bullshit narrative they've been spewing, didn't you? Girl slapping a hand to her mouth after you removed the mask, gasping and declaring: "Oh my God, it's him! The counselor who escaped the sanitarium!" or some shit like that.*)

I shrug again. *Would have been kinda cool.*

(*The cost of going off script.*)

Yeah.

(*Speaking of that final girl…*)

THE TRACK

God, I love him, Angela grinned to herself.

Eleanor Flynn pushed back her chair and stood with a speed that belied her seventy-plus years. "He's on to us," she said.

Angela laughed. It was now her turn to say: "*And?*"

Eleanor spun towards Stiles. "He's clearly on to us. We have to do something."

Angela didn't give Stiles a chance to reply. "When I mentioned that before, you didn't seem to have a care in the world about it. Now that it looks like my pony might be on to something, that something possibly culminating with the elimination of your hunter—the remaining killer *is* your hunter, yes?—then you're suddenly concerned."

Eleanor said nothing to Angela. Just kept her gaze on Stiles, waiting on his reply.

Stiles, hands steepled beneath his chin, glanced over at Eleanor with only his eyes. "I'd have to agree with Miss Thorne on this one, Eleanor. Your behavior is hypocritical."

Multiple facelifts and endless vials of Botox were helpless to the flush of agitation that reddened Eleanor's cheeks. "Well, then we at least need to warn the director," she said. "Let him know that—"

"The director will get no such call," Stiles interrupted. "If he happens to come by the knowledge of what's happening from his cast or on his own, fine; he may do as he wishes. But in the meantime, I for one am very eager to see how this plays out."

Eleanor sat back down in a huff, lips that were already thin now gone with contempt. Angela had been correct; the remaining killer *was* her hunter. Clearly, she did not want to lose him. For members of The Track, money was disposable; good hunters were not. With Calvin proving to be one hell of a pony, it was looking likely that Eleanor's hunter might be going the way of the dollar.

A part of Angela wished the old Calvin was back just then. She wanted to fuck him silly. Reward him as she'd always done in the past. Reward them *both*. Bringing Calvin in as her pony had come with sacrifices, chief of them being she hadn't been able to find herself a good lay since their last encounter. She wondered whether, since his instincts to survive were clearly still there, his instincts to fuck as well as he did would surface too. She could sneak into The Stable, visit him in his cell for one hell of a big surprise. Except two problems presented themselves with such a plan:

One, there was always the chance that his seeing her in the flesh might jog his memory. And if a mere glimpse didn't, her screwing his brains out would almost assuredly jar something loose; he was a hopeless addict in his past life, his drug of choice her flesh.

And two, wasn't the sex equal parts cerebral and physical for her? Physically, he performed well, but didn't she enjoy it that much more, both of them knowing that she was controlling and manipulating him with her sexual prowess as pathologically as the dealer governs the addict?

The mere thought of such exploitation and power made her tingle. Add Calvin's cock to the mix and she might damn well come the moment he was inside her.

Fucking sacrifices.

Stiles turned the volume up more so. Members locked in on their preferred monitor. The final act, as witnessed by members of The Track through various remote feeds...

Carly, tied to a chair inside the killer's cabin, grew impatient. The actors scattered about on the cabin floor playing dead, more so. One complained his face was stuck to the cabin floor in a now-dried pool of fake blood. Another, positioned awkwardly, complained her leg was falling asleep. A third complained she had to pee.

Carly called over her shoulder: "Maybe the other hunter got him."

The killer stepped out of the shadows into the dim and wavering candlelight. He spoke low and cautiously. "The director would have contacted us. Can I suggest you all shut up now? I have it on good authority that in addition to Greg, Courtney has recently broken character too, and both have now been punished."

A female voice rising amongst the bodies on the floor: "*Punished? Punished how?*"

The killer said nothing.

A male voice now rising amongst the bodies. "Yeah—punished how?"

"Fucking actors…" the killer muttered.

A rattle behind all of them. Someone trying to open the deliberately locked door: an unspoken cue for everyone to get back into character, for the killer to resume hiding in the shadows.

Except returning to such stations proved unnecessary. A knocking at the door was followed by a strong male voice calling: "*Open up! Show's over! I got him!*"

A collective sigh amongst the actors as they began to rise from their spots, the guy with his face stuck in a pool of fake blood whining as he peeled his cheek away, the girl with the sleepy leg shaking it out, the girl who had to pee rocking from foot to foot mumbling about finding a toilet, Carly asking to be untied, glad to be done with it all.

The final hunter pulled off his mask and watched them with clear disdain. Hunters seldom liked actors; the two were cut from entirely different cloths.

The hunter went to the door, unlocked and opened it. Calvin, wearing the previous hunter's mask and still carrying the machete, stepped inside and nodded hellos at the group.

"So, you got him?" the male actor who'd peeled his cheek from the floor asked as he attempted to wipe the sticky substance off his face.

"Yep," Calvin said.

"Shame," Carly said. "He was kinda cute."

"Yeah?" Calvin said.

"I thought so."

"Good to know." Calvin turned towards the hunter. "We the last two?"

The hunter nodded.

"Nice." Calvin whipped the machete into the neck of the final hunter, the scene playing out like the previous one, the machete only going in halfway, robbing Calvin of a clean beheading, the hunter dropping and gurgling and dying.

Every actor backed away as though the scene before them had erupted into a blazing fire. Half of them screamed.

Calvin yanked the machete from the dead hunter's neck, turned back towards the group, and pulled off his mask. "Ta da," he said. He then began a series of small, rapid-fire spits as though a bug had flown into his mouth. "Ugh…that mask had the last guy's blood in it. Now, *that's* commitment to the craft. You guys can appreciate that, yeah?"

Nobody said a word. Nobody seemed remotely capable.

"What's the matter, you guys got stage fright?" He laughed at his own joke.

"You…you know?" Carly managed.

"What I *know* is that it's fucking hard as hell to cut a dude's head off with one swipe of a machete. That's something you guys might have to figure out for your next production. I mean, sure, Greg's—or, should I say, *Anthony's*—came off easy, but he was a skinny guy, wasn't he?"

"*You killed Anthony?!*" someone blurted.

"*Me?* No. One of the masked dudes did." He mimed the action with his machete, finishing the act with a *pop!* sound. "Thing came right off."

"Anthony's *dead*?" another asked.

"Very. Courtney too."

"*What?!*"

Calvin frowned, waved the point of his machete between the group. "Why do you guys look so shocked? Aren't you are all part of the same fucked-up crew?"

Once again, they seemed incapable of response.

Calvin shrugged, looked at Carly, and said, "So you think I'm cute, huh?" before dropping instantly, his body rigid and seizing on the floor before going limp and unconscious…

Angela brandished the thumb drive-sized collar before the table. "I figured that was a good time," she said.

Stiles stood and performed a soft clap. "Bravo, Miss Thorne. Bravo."

The rest of the table followed suit. Even Eleanor, though her actions were clearly labored. First Tom Neil, now Eleanor. How long until the rest of the table resented her success? Stiles, even? Assuming they didn't already, that is.

DAYS LATER...

Angela Thorne wandered into the kitchen that was responsible for preparing the meals for all the ponies in The Stable. She recognized all but one staffer. And it was that one she had business with.

"Hi."

The young man, dressed in chef whites, heavily tattooed, long dark hair pulled back into a ponytail, whisking what looked to be eggs in a large metal bowl, did a double-take when he glanced up at Angela—first take: annoyance; second take: lust.

"Hi yourself," he said. He looked her up and down, all but licking his lips.

"You new here?" Angela asked.

"I am—yeah. Noticed me, huh?"

"When did you get here?"

The guy set the bowl aside and leaned against the table, showing off his muscular, tattooed forearms. He grinned. "Just in time, if you ask me."

"What happened to the guy you replaced?"

"Huh?"

"Earl. Old guy who used to putter around here. It occurred to me that I hadn't seen him in a while. What happened to him?"

"Hell, I don't know. Maybe he died."

Angela considered him a moment. "Maybe he did."

He returned a curious little frown. "Yeah, well—his loss; my gain."

"Your gain, huh? You get paid that well?"

His curious frown remained. "It's all right."

"I wonder…if a man like you could be persuaded to do a little something extra for the right price."

"If the currency is you sitting on my face, I might."

Angela stared at him without blinking.

He looked away. Began fidgeting on the spot. "What the hell do you want, lady?"

"Pony Twenty-two. Tell me, what do you plan on putting in his juice cup today, hmmm?"

SURGERY

Angela stepped into the operating room and found Dr. Adesida scrubbing up at the sink, his back to her. Two assistants organizing instruments flanked him.

"Doctor," Angela said. "Getting ready to perform another shitty implant?"

The two assistants stopped their prep instantly and faced Angela.

Dr. Adesida, however, did not flinch. He continued washing his hands, calmly replying to Angela over his shoulder.

"I was told there was a chance you might be coming by, Miss Thorne." Despite decades in the United States, Dr. Adesida's West African accent was still evident. *There* was *dere*. *Thorne* was *Dorne*.

"Is it possible maybe you were expecting me even before you were warned?" Angela said.

Dr. Adesida snatched a paper towel from the dispenser, dried his hands, and finally faced her. Dr. Adesida was short and very thin. His most striking features were his exceptionally pale blue eyes, their contrast with his dark skin almost hypnotic at first glance.

"Insinuating what, by chance?" he asked.

"That you botched my pony's implant on purpose," Angela replied flatly.

The two assistants exchanged an awkward glance. "Should we leave, Dr. Adesida?" one of them asked.

His milky blue eyes stayed fixed on Angela when he replied to them. "No—please carry on as you were. Miss Thorne, what possible motive would I have for spoiling your pony's implant?"

"Biggest motive there is. Money."

"I have enough wealth for ten lifetimes, Miss Thorne. Ten *extravagant* lifetimes."

"Your life, then," she said.

The doctor chuckled genuinely. "Do you know where we are, Miss Thorne? The people we work for? They do not threaten; they *do*. If they wanted your pony's implantation to be…"—he circled his hand, searching for the appropriate word—"*compromised*, they would not need to threaten. They would not even ask. They would tell."

"Fair enough. Did any members of The Track *tell* you to mess with my pony's implant?"

Dr. Adesida chuckled genuinely again. "I only take instruction from the senior-most members of The Track." *The Track* was *De Drack*.

"And are they somehow exempt from such unscrupulousness? Do you know where we are, Dr. Adesida? The people we work for?" Her delight in serving his words back to him was evident.

Dr. Adesida appeared curiously delighted as well. Amused by her condescending wit. "I am handling your pony's procedure this afternoon, Miss Thorne. It is the standard Stable implantation to return his memory to that of a prison inmate. He has handled it well before, but if you are doubting my scruples, you are more than welcome to observe the operation."

Angela's tone still held notes of condescension when she replied: "Considerate of you, but I'm afraid it would be the equivalent of your translating foreign direction to me—I would have absolutely no way of knowing if what you were interpreting was genuine…until after the fact, that is." She licked her lips. "Should I be concerned that your directions will get me lost, Dr. Adesida?"

He smiled. "You're here now, Miss Thorne."

"I am, yes. Please carry on with my pony's procedure as planned."

He gave a slight bow of the head. "Of course."

THE STABLE

Boom of the heavy steel door at the far end of the corridor. Lights flickering before exploding to life and momentarily blinding me. Breakfast. Guard on his way.

Except no always-squeaking wheels of the cart carrying my breakfast. No clacks of the guard's boots on concrete growing closer.

I kick off my blanket and roll out of bed. I approach the bars and mash my face against them to try to get a look down the far end of the corridor, to see what's what.

I see nothing. Still hear nothing.

"*Hello?*" I call. "Someone there?"

And then there *is* a squeak. Not from a wheel, though. I look down, and a black kitten is in my cell, looking up at me with impossibly big yellow eyes.

Where the hell did *this* guy come from?

It squeaks up at me again. Sits back on its little butt and squeaks some more. I bend and pick it up. It purrs immediately and climbs onto my shoulder where it begins to nuzzle into the side of my face, its purring louder in my ear.

I can't help but smile. "Where did you come from, little guy?"

Wait—*is* it a guy?

I pluck him off my shoulder and check his rear end. I see a tiny set of furry black balls. Yep.

I place him back on my shoulder and stroke his chin with two fingers. "Sorry about that."

His purring grows stronger than ever, almost as if to say, *no worries, man.* He then gives a playful little nip to my cheek as though to add, *you only get one of those, though.*

I get close to the bars again, kitten still on my shoulder.

"*Hello?!*" I call again.

Still I hear nothing. I did hear the unmistakable boom of the heavy cell block door open and close, though. And the lights did come on in the entire block.

(*Can't the two things be mutually exclusive?*)

Not in my experience. Maybe they started to wheel in breakfast and then got hung up?

(*Or maybe they let the kitten in.*)

The kitten was already in my cell, wasn't he? He had to be. If someone tossed in a kitten at the end of the block, I would have spotted it wandering towards me. This little guy—I stroke his chin with two fingers again—*appeared out of nowhere.*

(*You saying someone put him in here while you were sleeping?*)

I can't think of any other explanation.

(*Why the hell would they give you a kitten?*)

I take the kitten over to my cot and sit down, now placing him on my lap. He instantly curls up into a fuzzy black ball and sacks out. My heart swells.

A sudden flash of light jolts my head like a punch. I cry out and grip my head with one hand.

The fuck was that?!

I look down at the kitten. He's still zonked, undisturbed by—

A second flash of light. I pluck the kitten off my lap and toss him onto my cot before dropping to my knees on my cell floor. My head pounds as though my brain is expanding, keen on cracking my skull. Worse still, images flash against the screens of my tightly shut eyelids, demanding to be seen.

I see a cat. A black cat. Bigger than the kitten. Full grown. I'm sitting somewhere with him on my lap, stroking his chin with two fingers just as

I was the kitten moments ago. My heart swells more so from the memory, battling the agonizing swelling in my head.

Another flash of an image. Me handing the black cat over to someone. A woman. The love is now a painful love. A lost love. I'm giving the cat away. Why? Why would I give him away if I love him so much?

A third flash. The cat looking at me as I hand him over to the woman. His face, assuredly no different to the onlooker, is different to me. He's confused. He can sense my pain. His big yellow eyes asking me, *What's going on? Why are you crying? Are you giving me away? Are you leaving me? Why are you leaving me?*

"*GET OUT!*" I scream to my head, to these memories that can't be, *can't be* mine. "*GET THE FUCK OUT!*"

"*Twenty-two!*"

I look up. The guard is looking down at me from behind the cell bars, the cart with my breakfast next to him.

"*What the fuck are you doing?*" he asks.

I gape around for a spell, mouth open, like a kid who stumbled onto a nude beach.

I'm on all fours on the floor of my prison cell.

Was I dreaming? Sleepwalking? I don't remember—

"What, were you praying to Allah or something?" he says, laughing at his own wit. His smile then drops like a stone as his eyes fix on something behind me. "*What the hell is that?*"

I follow his gaze and look behind me. The kitten is there. Curled up and asleep on my pillow.

That's right—I found a kitten in my cell. That much I remember.

Still on my knees, I turn back to the guard. "I don't know. It was here this morning when I woke up."

He pulls a face. "*What?*"

I get to my feet. My head throbs. "Like I said, it was here when I woke up."

The guard sticks his arm through the bars. "Hand it over."

I look back at the kitten. He's still ridiculously zonked. A bomb could go off, and I don't think he would wake. I turn back towards the guard. "Why?"

"What do you mean *why*?" He thrusts his arm farther between the bars, hand splayed demonstratively. "*Give it to me.*"

I look back at the kitten again, and he's suddenly awake, sitting up on my pillow and looking into me with those big yellow eyes as though asking me if I'm going to give him away.

My eyes fill with tears. I've known this cat for all of five minutes, and my fucking eyes fill with tears at the thought of giving him away. Makes no sense.

I turn back to the guard. "No."

"*Excuse me?*"

"I said no. I'm keeping him."

"You are, huh? Twenty-two, I'm going to give you just five seconds to place that cat in my hand right—"

Without thinking, I grab his wrist and yank him towards me, his face banging hard against the bars, knees buckling beneath him.

I let go, and he drops to his knees, clutching his face, moaning and cursing my name. He soon shakes away the stars, gets to his feet, shakes his head a bit more, and then looks at me with murder in his eyes.

"You know, I was told to let you keep it. *I* wanted to see you beg a little first, but I *was* gonna let you keep it in the end. But after that shit you just pulled? There's no fucking *way* you're keeping that thing now."

I show him my palms. "I'm sorry, man, okay? I'm sorry. I don't know what happened, I just got—"

"Too late for begging now, you son of a bitch." He goes into his pocket and holds up a tiny little device between his thumb and index finger. It looks like a thumb drive. "When you wake, kitty will be long gone. Scratch that—kitty will be long *dead*. Nighty-night, asshole."

⸱   ⸱   ⸱

Boom of the heavy steel door at the far end of the corridor. Lights flickering before exploding to life. Breakfast. Guard on his way.

I feel something on my chest, look down, and see there's a black kitten curled up and sleeping on me. What the hell?

"Morning, Twenty-two," the guard says. It's a different guy this time. Not the usual asshole.

"Morning," I say, still flat on my cot. I scratch the kitten beneath its chin with two fingers. It begins to purr. The sound is like a calming drug to me.

"How's the little fella doing today?" the guard asks.

I have absolutely no fucking idea what is going on. Yet still I manage: "He's good."

"You know, I'd be in deep shit if anyone found out you had him in there with you."

I nod. "Yeah, I know. Thanks."

"Thought of a name for him yet?" he asks as he begins to get my breakfast tray sorted.

For some reason, I say: "Pele."

CLICHE
EPISODE THREE

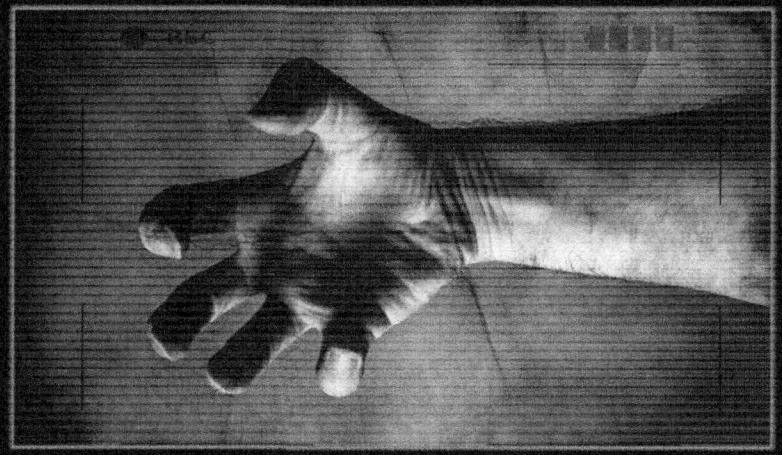

THE STABLE

The familiar boom of the heavy steel door at the far end of my cell block. Soles of the guard's shoes clacking against the concrete as he approaches. I hope it's the cool guard—the guard who lets me keep Pele without a word to anyone. Although I'm not sure why it wouldn't be; I haven't seen the asshole guard who'd threatened to take—no, *kill*—Pele the day I found him meowing his little head off in my cell. It's been how long? Couple of weeks? Maybe the asshole got fired. Fine by me.

New guy is cool. Even sneaks me treats for Pele. Helps me hide his litter box come inspection time. Although, have I ever had an inspection? I think so. My memory is kinda hazy right now. I can't even remember why I'm in prison; I just know I'm in prison. With my own private cell block to boot. I must have done something really bad to get my own private block. Is this death row? I never see any other inmates. I hear them sometimes, echoes of their hollers in the distance, but I never see them. Even during mandatory workout time, they make me train alone.

The mandatory workout thing is odd too. What the hell do they care if I stay fit? I don't mind it, of course—it's a nice stress reliever—but it's more than a little odd that it's mandatory and, again, solitary. Maybe they don't want me mixing with the other prisoners? Maybe I did something *really* bad and they fear for my life if they put me in general population? Oh fuck—was I a fucking pedophile or some sick shit? Why the fuck can't I remember?

No.

No, no, no—if I was a sick fuck like that, no way would the guard be so nice to me. Civil, maybe, but letting me keep Pele? Sneaking him treats, helping me hide his litter box, etcetera? No way is a guard doing that for a piece-of-shit pedophile. If only I could remember. I don't even remember how old I am.

"Hey, Twenty-two." It *is* the cool guard. He's standing in front of my cell, smiling genuinely. He's got something in his right hand: a Styrofoam cup with a lid, with what looks to be some kind of meat wrapped in plastic wrap perched on top of the cup. "Nearly lights-out." He raises the Styrofoam cup topped with mystery meat. "Got a bedtime snack for Mr. Pele."

I look behind me. Pele is sawing toothpicks on my pillow—a furry black ball of pure contentment. I love the little fucker more than I've ever…well…I don't know whether I've ever loved anyone. But I know I love him. I look back to the guard.

"You're too freaking cool, man," I say. "I can't thank you enough for all you've done in helping me keep him a secret."

"My pleasure, Twenty-two. Always was a sucker for animals."

"The last guard threatened to kill him." Something suddenly comes back to me. "No, wait—he said he was told to let me keep him first. I think. My memory's been weird lately. I'm pretty sure he said he was told to let me keep him, but he wanted to fuck with me a little first, make me beg. Like an idiot, I pulled his outstretched arm through the bars and nearly knocked him cold."

Cool guard chuckles, which I find odd. You would think there would be some kind of fraternity thing between them.

"That's when he threatened to kill him," I went on. "Next thing I know, I'm waking up with Pele asleep on my chest and you're there, asking me how the little guy is doing." I pause a moment, trying to work it all out. My memory of that seems clear, only it doesn't make much sense. It's like I lost time somewhere. Or maybe imagined it? Dreamt it?

"Must have dreamt that," the guard says, as though reading my mind. "Mike—the guard before me—was transferred months ago. I've been your guard for a while now. Certainly since Pele came on the scene."

Couldn't be a dream; I remember it too clearly. "Are you sure? Seems so vivid in my mind."

"Pretty sure I would have heard about you attacking a fellow officer."

Hard to argue with that. "I suppose."

"You want this or what?" he asks, holding up the cup.

"Sure."

He hands it through the bars. I take the meat in plastic wrap off the top and place it on the solitary table in my cell. I raise the cup. "This milk?"

"No—that's for you." He winks at me.

I frown, open the lid, and smell the brown liquid inside. It's whiskey. "What the hell is this?"

"You don't want it?"

"No, no, I do—it's just…why are you giving me whiskey?"

"Said you had trouble sleeping the past few nights. Thought this might help. Don't tell anyone."

"I said that?"

"Sure did. Wow—your memory really is fucked, isn't it?"

"Yeah, it is. Can't even remember how old I am. My own birthday."

"Mine's coming up. August 18th. August 18th, 1973, to be exact."

On the afternoon of August 18, 1973, five young people in a Volkswagen van ran out of gas on a farm road in South Texas. Four of them were never seen again…

A blinding white light singes my eyes. My head throbs. I cry out and clamp my hands over both temples, shutting my eyes tight against the pain.

"Hey! Hey, you all right, Twenty-two?"

The pain is gone as quickly as it arrived. I open my eyes slowly and can only stare back at the guard, dumbfounded.

"You all right?" he asks again. "What happened?"

I shake my head. "No idea. Something came back to me just now."

"What did?"

"I don't know—I can't remember it now. Your birthday…it triggered the memory."

He laughs. "*Chainsaw* fan?"

"Huh?"

"My birthday," he says. "It's the same fictional date from the film *The Texas Chainsaw Massacre*. I get that sometimes from diehard fans."

Another flash of light, this one not as blinding, this one projecting something in my mind's eye:

I'm sitting on a sofa, drinking whiskey, watching *The Texas Chainsaw Massacre*, chasing the whiskey with pills. Why chasing with pills? Trying to kill myself? The opening monologue by a young John Larroquette plays; however, it is *not* the same monologue that flashed into my mind moments ago. The original *Chainsaw* monologue did not mention the date of August 18th, 1973—the sequel did, of which I am also a fan.

At least I think I am.

More comes back to me:

The opening sequence in *Chainsaw* one. Flash photos of a corpse The Hitchhiker dug up to ultimately be mounted on a monument in a cemetery. *God, I love this film*, I can remember thinking, remember taking more pills, more whiskey, Jim Beam to be exact.

I look up at the guard again, still no blinding light, no headache as before, just fragmented memories belonging to me? Must be me, right? I gesture to the whiskey. "Is that Jim Beam?"

He gives a curious frown. "Matter of fact, it is. How did you know that?"

I don't answer, just shut my eyes again, and the memory resumes:

I take the last of the pills. Things are getting fuzzy. I want to see Leatherface. I want to see what I think is the best scene in cinematic history. I want to see when Leatherface hits Kirk with the sledgehammer, drags him inside, and then slams the steel door shut with the boom to end all booms.

And then it's all gone.

I look up at the guard, and I'm sure my face is that of a child's, a boy who has the audacity to ask for more, despite the frightening prospects that loom.

Dickens, anyone?

Who? Was he a character in *Chainsaw* too?

"Twenty-two," the guard says. "Are you all right, man?"

"I think…I think I *am* a fan," I say.

"Of *Chainsaw* or Jim Beam?"

"Both, I think."

"Well, then drink up quick and give me back the cup before I get shit for giving it to you."

I nod and gulp the cup in three big swallows, grimacing from its bite, yet keeping it down all the same.

"Impressive," he says.

I hand him back the cup. The whiskey is already warming my belly and easing my mind. It's a comfortable, familiar feeling. Like a hug capable of taking a shit day away. What I'd give for some more.

Please, sir, can I have some more?

Dickens.

Who??

Christ, my mind is a mess. I shake my head and clear the cobwebs.

"Don't forget Pele's treat," he says, gesturing behind me. "Don't want him going all MMA on your ass."

"Huh?"

"MMA? Mixed martial arts? Didn't you name him Pele after Jose 'Pele' Landi-Jons? Your favorite fighter?"

"Did I?"

"That's what you told me."

"I told you that?"

"You really are out of it, aren't you?"

Jose "Pele" Landi-Jons?

Sudden flash of a sinewy black guy clamping onto the back of another dude's neck and kneeing him in the face. This happening in some kind of cage.

My headache comes back with a vengeance, the blinding light, the works. I shut my eyes tight again and pray for the pain to subside. It eventually does, and I will myself not to remember any more. Remembering equals pain. Ignorance, as they say, is bliss—at least for me, it would seem

"Jesus, man," the guard says, "let that whiskey do its thing and get some sleep. Maybe you'll remember more in the morning."

No thanks. Ignorance is bliss is my new motto. Still, I say: "Thanks."

He turns and leaves.

I look back at Pele. He's still zonked on my pillow. I don't have the heart to wake him, even for food. I'll give it to him in the morning. For now, I stuff the wrapped meat—pork? Chicken? Looks like pork—under my mattress and then get into bed, resting my head next to Pele. I give him a two-fingered pet on the top of his head just the way he likes, and though his eyes don't open, he begins his trademark buzz saw—

Buzz saw.

Chainsaw.
On the afternoon of August 18th, 1973…
STOP!
—purr and the sound beats any amount of Jim Beam—
"*Is that Jim Beam?*" "*Matter of fact it is. How did you know that?*"
—any day. I'm asleep in seconds.

⁂

The man was waiting for Officer Hall the moment he exited Calvin's cell block.

"Everything go all right?" The man was meticulously dressed and groomed. Suit and haircut more than Hall made in six months. Only blemish was a small white scar running through his left eyebrow.

"Smooth as always," Hall said, holding out his hand.

The man handed over the ritual envelope of cash involving such matters. Hall took it and stuffed it into his back pocket. "You know if the big dogs ever cottoned on to what you were doing…"

The man waved a dismissive hand at Hall. "My concern; not yours."

"They've got cameras everywhere."

"Again; my concern."

"I'm just saying; fucking with a pony like this—it's not like they'd just give us a pink slip. We'd end up like poor Mike. Guy was an asshole, but he didn't deserve to—"

"*I* took care of Mike. The Track knows nothing about it."

"You keep saying 'I,'" Hall said. "Shouldn't you just be saying 'we?'"

"If you're digging, I suggest you stop," the man said. "That is, of course, unless you want your newfound income to stop."

Hall buttoned his lip with his thumb and index finger.

The man nodded once. "Wise."

"So, we done then?" Hall asked.

"Until next time."

THE TRACK

All members of The Track took their seats at the large rectangular table in the center of the room and readied themselves for the standard formalities that preceded each new Cliché on deck.

All members but one. And Angela Thorne immediately took notice.

"Smells nice in here," she said. "We missing an asshole?"

The table murmured confusion, the joke whizzing past their heads.

Robert Stiles, senior-most member of The Track, seventy, gaunt and gray, zillionaire, spoke from his spot at the head of the table. The joke did not miss him.

"Tom has chosen to sit this Cliché out, Miss Thorne. And your schoolyard wit is best left in such a place. No one is amused."

Angela held up a hand. "My apologies. It won't happen again."

Stiles's remark was not too far off: schoolyard behavior was exactly what had taken place between Tom Neil and Angela over the course of the past two Clichés involving Angela's pony. Tom Neil resenting Angela's success as a newcomer to The Track, Angela gloating Tom Neil's way with none too much subtlety over that success.

Tom Neil had even been asked to leave for inappropriate conduct during the last outing that eventually saw Angela's pony prevail once again. It surprised Angela, and it didn't when she did not see Tom in attendance today: Her pony, Calvin, was on deck to perform. She would have thought he'd be first in attendance, hoping beyond hope to watch her pony fail.

Or perhaps such a fragile ego, as Tom Neil clearly had, could not tolerate watching Angela's pony—or, more aptly, Angela herself—prevail yet again. Yes, such a porcelain ego in the likes of Tom Neil was more likely to opt for forfeit than to endure another loss. Had her schoolyard quip not been chastised moments ago, she might have coughed out "*pussy!*", only to admit to herself that such a remark would not have been nearly as delightful without Tom himself in attendance to swallow it.

"Thank you," Stiles said. "Shall we begin?" he asked Angela, the entire table.

Angela nodded with the rest of the table.

The remote was handed down to Angela. She hit the appropriate button, "spun the wheel," and each pair of eyes present chose their preferred monitor lining the walls (dozens, large and small, pristine in their clarity and design) to watch with bated breath for which particular Cliché would present itself for Angela's pony on this day.

The flashing list of options, hundreds of them, all of them gracing the screen for less than a second like code being uploaded, far too fast for any human eye to trace, ultimately slowed before landing on one. And, as was typically the case whenever *any* Cliché was displayed, the table *oohed* excitedly in unison. It was not the content of the Cliché that so tickled members of The Track—although some particular Clichés *were* more arousing than others—but rather the metaphorical Christmas Eve of the whole thing; it never failed to tickle their desires. Kids waiting for Santa, all of them. If Santa was bringing them carnage, that is. And he was.

ZOMBIE APOCALYPSE, the monitor read.

Eleanor Flynn, another senior member, another billionaire, whose contempt for Angela's success (she'd lost a hunter to Angela's pony on the past outing) may not have been as blatant as Tom Neil's, but still flashed from time to time, even under the seemingly composed face that was aided by facelifts and Botox and whatever black-market substance—a child's *foreskin*, Angela had once heard; how the hell did *that* work?—she could afford (and she could) that allowed her advancing age to hit as many roadblocks as possible, gave an uncharacteristic whistle. *Sucks to be you*, that whistle said to Angela.

Robert Stiles glanced over at Eleanor. She glanced back. His reprimand to her was a long blink, his reprimand of choice to veterans of The Track who had forgotten their place.

Eleanor accepted Stiles's silent rebuke with a single nod and placed her attention back on Angela.

And Angela, for all her trademark confidence, looked momentarily flustered.

"A zombie apocalypse?" she said. "Just how the heck are you going to pull that off?"

"Never a good idea to peek behind the curtain, Miss Thorne," Stiles said. "Suffice to say, we have pulled it off multiple times before."

Angela did not doubt this. The Track's resources were limitless. She would, in fact, not be surprised if The Track had *actual* zombies stowed away somewhere for this particular scenario. But still...

"How?" she asked. "I mean...*zombies*?"

"My word on prior successes with this particular scenario should be all the reassurance you need, Miss Thorne. That is, of course, unless you are once again questioning procedure—don't think your little conversation with Doctor Adesida went unheard."

Angela had confronted one of The Track's primary surgeons, Doctor Adesida, following Calvin's last Cliché. She'd suggested an intentional botch-job on Calvin's implant that made surviving his Cliché harder than it need be. And while her conversation with Doctor Adesida had been private, or at least was meant to be, Angela had no qualms about blurting to members of The Track before ultimately confronting the doctor that something frankly stunk during Calvin's past outing, that someone was deliberately trying to sabotage her pony.

"I'm not questioning procedure, I just want to know—"

Stiles held up his bony hand, silencing her. "I will offer you the same deal I offered you when you were seemingly dissatisfied with the last Cliché your pony was slated to take part in. Do you remember what that was?"

"I remember. Either forfeit now and leave The Track forever—forever meaning dead—or allow Calvin to proceed as is."

Stiles gave his solitary long blink. "I don't recall using such words."

"You didn't need to; they were sufficiently implied."

"Your interpretation of my proposal is your own; you're free to take it as you will. But the same offer stands today. You may pull your pony and forfeit the day—"

Forfeit like Tom Neil? Not a fucking chance.

"—as a result of which your membership to The Track will be removed, along with your tongue concerning the goings-on within The Track—"

Ah, there's that not-so-subtle threat again.

"—or you may wish to keep your pony on deck and prepare for the day's event. Perhaps even gain a little confidence that Doctor Adesida's implantation for this particular Cliché will go as well as all the others he has performed, countless times, over the years."

Angela smiled. "Option B, please."

"Excellent," Stiles said. "May I also remind you that I have placed money on your pony, placed money and *won*, on his past two outings? If such a concern over the prospect of someone attempting to sabotage your pony appeared evident to more than you—to me specifically—I hardly would have placed such sizable bets on him"

"You have lifetimes of money to burn," Angela said, before instantly regretting it.

Stiles did not appear annoyed this time. "True," he said. "To many, money is superfluous at The Track. It is the show—the hunt—that we all prize."

The table nodded and murmured agreement. Stiles went on.

"But money is money, Miss Thorne. And as I believe you and I have discussed before, along with the delight of a good show comes the elation of victory should the pony we backed win the day."

Hard to argue with that. Winning was nice. But so was money. Angela liked both. More so, she loved power. And hadn't her past conversation with Stiles involved that last thing? Power? How someone might sabotage a pony, not for money or the thrill of victory, but to ultimately usurp Stiles at the head of the table? To rule The Track one day? The methods of fucking with the system in order to achieve those means were many, sabotaging ponies being only one of them.

But still, even Stiles himself had mentioned the faintest lack of trust in the air at The Track, how he was sure someone would love to take his seat one day, perhaps sooner than later. In that, Stiles very much appeared the mob boss who keeps his men happy, but not too happy, and who is not above making an example of them should they begin courting delusions of usurpation (see: the recent not-so-subtle threat about losing one's tongue should Angela forfeit). Hell, for all Angela knew, Tom Neil was dead after routinely stepping out of line during Calvin's previous outing, and she was the only one who hadn't heard about it yet.

Yes, power, Angela believed, surpassed the blessed hunt in desirability. Surpassed victory. Certainly surpassed what was disposable income for all of them.

Angela only smiled and again said: "Option B, please."

Now Stiles smiled, the faintest crinkle on the corner of his thin mouth. "Thank you. And though I have no obligation to tell you as such, I plan to put another sizable bet on your pony to prevail today."

Bully for you.

"Good luck," Angela said.

Stiles addressed the rest of the table. "What's the cap on hunters for this one?"

"A lot," a woman three seats from Angela said. "Seven, I believe."

Eleanor Flynn whistled again.

Stiles gave his long blink her way again.

"You running low, Eleanor?" Angela asked, alluding to Calvin burying a machete in the neck of one of her hunters during his past outing, a clichéd take on slasher films from the eighties.

Eleanor clearly struggled to remain composed in the face of Angela's cheek.

And wasn't it more than just Angela's cheek and the loss of her hunter to Angela's pony that Eleanor resented? Was it not Angela's beauty, which Eleanor no doubt secretly coveted, that made Angela's cheek and past victories sting that much more? All the child foreskins in the world could never bring her to Angela's level in that department.

The Tom Neils of the world—pathetic as they were—would always fall victim to their fragile egos in the presence of powerful and assured women. Yet the Eleanor Flynns of the world were, in Angela's experience, far more pathetic. Their contempt primarily resulted from the superficial insecurity that resided in almost all women while in the presence of a superior beauty of the same sex—the new girl at school who is secretly hissed at by her peers as she strolls on by. Indeed, women were far worse than men in this regard, and it delighted Angela to no end. *I've got something you can never buy, bitch, and I'll remind you of it often*—this thought culminating with the flash of a perfect smile on a perfect face with even the faintest bat of perfect eyelashes Eleanor's way.

"Oh no, Miss Thorne," Eleanor replied. "I have plenty. I'd like to enlist three."

The table murmured excitedly.

Eleanor's move, her brazen enlisting of three hunters, was meant to project confidence. Angela, who had a dog's gift for smelling fear, bought it like email spam, and smiled that perfect smile Eleanor's way again.

"That leaves four more slots available," Stiles said. "If you're interested, speak now."

Hunters were hired. Bets were placed. Producers, directors, and actors were hired.

Angela thought: *Nothing to do now but adjourn and reassemble once we get notice that Calvin's implant has been successfully performed—when he'll wake to find himself in the ridiculous predicament of a zombie fucking apocalypse.*

THE SET

A sinking feeling. Like…like I'm drowning? Do I know what drowning feels like?

Maybe I do. I don't know. I don't know much. What I *do* know is that the feeling is not one of panic, as I'm sure drowning almost assuredly feels, but one of peace. The feeling one gets moments before slowly drifting off to sleep.

Drift. Yes, that seems apt. No, wait—not drift. Sink, remember? Sinking. I'm *sinking*, the view above me growing darker as I slowly descend into the black below.

I can see light above

Go to the light! Isn't that what they always say?

but the light above, narrowing, growing dimmer as I descend, feels like too much effort. I *want* to sink into the black below.

The black below feels welcoming, comforting, like that aforementioned feeling of drifting off to sleep. I don't want to go to the light. Something inside of me—I don't know what—is telling me the light equals pain. The light is not a pleasant place to be. People who want to fight for their lives *want* to go to the light, but not me. I want to drop deeper into the black, to sink into nothingness and be done with it all. I want to go to sleep forever. I don't know much, not much at all in fact, but I do know this. There is a depression inside of me that is the only true sensation I can feel. It feels hardwired; the will to fight and prevail and conquer such a feeling is a fight long lost in me. Again, I don't know much, but of this feeling I'm sure.

So, I'm not going to fight it. I'm going to sink. I'm going to sink and sink until the light above is gone and all around me is black, where nothing will bother me anymore and I can sleep forever. That's what I want.

It would seem, however, that my body is at war with my mind, as my descent, despite my will to keep it going, has stopped, and now I am rising towards the light against my will.

Why? I don't want to fucking rise. Just let me sink. Let me sleep forever. Please.

And then it occurs to me: someone is bringing me towards the light. Someone is…calling to me? It is faint and nearly indistinct, but it's there. It's a number.

Twenty-two?

They are not calling my name,

(*what* is *my name?*)

but it feels certain they *are* calling to me, whoever they might be. And they are calling me by a number: the number twenty-two, its faintness rising in clarity as I rise. Rising towards that goddamn light—

"*Wake up, Twenty-two!*"

—that bright fucking light that is now beginning to find its way through my eyelids as I am about to surface. And as I begin to surface, I can feel that lovely ocean of black I so want to descend back into grow rough and choppy. It is shaking me, jostling me, as though someone is in that black ocean with me, trying to pull me to the surface completely. To save me.

I open my eyes. The light above is brutal. I'm momentarily blind and shut my eyes tight. Purple and yellow stars give a fireworks display on the canvas that is my eyelids. I hear shuffling around me, like hurried feet. Hurried feet on the water?

But of course I'm not in the water. Never was. Still blind, I can only feel around me to determine my surroundings. I'm in a bed—I feel sheets, blankets, a pillow behind my head. I was asleep. Fuck. How I hoped I really was drowning. Even though I am now awake, the urge to be anything but is still very much with me….

Me.

Me?

Now there's a question that should take precedence over any and all. *Who is me?*

I open my eyes again. A squint at first. Then a little more at a time until everything settles. The light above me is fluorescent. Rectangles of fluorescence among rectangles of ceiling tiles. I'm definitely not in my bed. But then, where *is* my bed?

I look around me. One doesn't need to have ever been in a hospital to know he is in one now, that I'm in one now.

An accident? Was I in an accident? Is that why I can't remember anything? A head injury, maybe? Amnesia?

"Hello?" I call, and my head instantly throbs. Yes, a head injury seems likely. Or it could be residual effects from the blinding light above. Either way, I close my eyes and try again: *"Hello?"*

I wait...and get nothing in return.

And the shuffling feet you heard moments ago? Someone must *be close.*

THE TRACK

MOMENTS AGO...

All members of The Track watched as Calvin lay in the hospital bed, unable to wake from sedation.

"Is he dead?" one member asked.

"His vitals appear fine," another responded, glancing at one of a handful of monitors that displayed as such.

"Comatose?" another suggested. "Couldn't handle the implant?"

Eleanor Flynn, with none too subtle delight Angela's way: "Wouldn't be the first time he struggled with implantation."

Angela, refusing to acknowledge Eleanor, looked directly at Stiles, and Stiles alone. "Give him time. He'll wake."

"And how long do you suggest we wait, Miss Thorne?" The question was clearly rhetorical. The Track didn't like to wait.

"Well, then can we wake him?" Angela said.

"The script calls for a deserted hospital," Eleanor said. "Shall we do rewrites? Set us back a day to accommodate your pony's lack of will?" This too was rhetorical. Such a prospect was out of the question.

Angela still refused to acknowledge Eleanor. Kept her gaze on Stiles.

Stiles pulled out his phone, called the director. "Wake him...yes, I'm well aware..." Stiles listened, gave his long blink. "Are you asking me how to do your job?" He listened some more. "Then do it, and please don't disappoint us."

Stiles hung up.

"What did he—?" Angela started, but got no further, Stiles's raised index finger cutting her off like a switch. He then gestured to the monitors with the same index finger. *Watch and see*, his gesture said.

Angela did watch, as did the rest of The Track.

They watched, no, *listened*, as a hospital intercom could be heard booming: "*Wake up, Twenty-two!*"

And when Calvin still would not stir, they *did* have something to watch—one of the director's assistants creeping into the hospital room, duck-walking below Calvin's line of sight from atop the hospital bed, reaching up blindly and grabbing hold of Calvin's shoulder, jostling him hard, registering that Calvin was finally beginning to wake, and then hurrying out in the same manner from which he entered, low and out of sight.

Calvin opened his eyes.

The table, save Eleanor Flynn, sighed relief.

"Seems as though your pony is always getting second chances," Eleanor said to Angela, alluding to Calvin's struggles with his implant during his past outing.

Angela's reply was a smile and brief scratch of her eye with her middle finger.

THE SET

"*Hellooooo….?*"

I wait. Still nothing.

I feel something by my right hand. A rectangular thing like a remote control. It's a nurse call device. I push the appropriate button. Wait and…

Nothing.

I push again and again, mashing the button on the last push. I can hear it buzzing somewhere in the distance of the hospital. Should I be able to hear that? Because I can't hear anything else but. Hospitals are a beehive of activity usually, yes?

I notice there is no IV in my right arm, no IV drip stand next to my bed. There should be one, shouldn't there?

Screw this. I get out of bed. I'm wearing a hospital gown, the kind where your ass has no place to hide. I look around the room to see whether I can spot clothing anywhere. I can't.

I check the solitary closet in the room. Here we go—a pair of jeans, a gray sweatshirt, boxers, socks, and shoes. I put them on, go to leave, and realize I need to take a wicked piss. I do so in my room's private bathroom, flush, wash my hands, and then leave the room and step out into the hallway.

It's empty. Like, really empty. It's something you can feel just as much as see. I think of the rapture, as though everyone ascended to heaven in a flash of light, leaving their stations as was: phones dropped and left dangling midcall, instruments clanging to the floor miduse, papers leaving hands that had suddenly vanished and seesawing slowly to the floor.

And so if it was the rapture, what does that make me? The one dude who didn't ascend? I still can't remember a thing, but if my butt stayed put here, in this abandoned hospital, I must have done some pretty nasty shit in my day.

But the hospital can't be abandoned. It can't be—I'm sure I heard someone in my room just before I woke. And the whole rapture nonsense is just that.

"HELLLOOOOO…????"

I get nothing but my own voice echoing back to me, the echo stronger than it should be due to the lack of occupants, no doubt. But again, there *has* to be occupants. How on earth can I be the only one here?

Voices in the distance prove me wrong.

I immediately follow them down the deserted hallway and hit what looks to be reception—a large semicircle of a desk with all things reception behind it. Among those things is a television perched up high behind that semicircle of a desk. There is no one behind the desk. No one close by. The voices are coming from the television. The station is a news channel. A banner scrolls across the bottom of the screen, stating one thing only, over and over: "*The dead are alive.*"

A female reporter elaborates: "Again, we cannot emphasize enough to stay in your homes, do *not* venture outside in an attempt to reach loved ones…"

What the fuck?

"…their numbers are growing, literally by the hour, and the Department of Homeland Security is struggling to…"

The dead walking the earth? Are you kidding me?

"…have assured us that this is *not* a terrorist threat, but something else entirely…something unfathomable. Again, do not attempt to…"

I'm still dreaming. I've got to be. Wake up. *Wake the fuck up.*

"…Armageddon over the course of the past several weeks…"

Several weeks??? I've been out cold for several weeks? Shouldn't I feel weaker? My muscles atrophied?

And how is there power in this place? The news lady said it's like Armageddon. So how is there still power in this place? And water too? The toilet I used in my room gave that industrial-strength flush exclusive to all industrial-strength johns. And I washed my hands after. No shortage of water there. If this was Armageddon, or—and I can't believe I'm saying this—some kind of zombie apocalypse, then wouldn't power and water be the first to go? No way FEMA would have it back up and running so fast, would they? With all the undead peeps to concern themselves with first?

"…taste for human flesh…"

Listen to yourself, man. Are you actually dissecting this? No way this is real. Has to be some kind of trick. Someone fucking with you.

(Someone who rented out an entire hospital to employ such a trick? Filmed a news segment and had it playing just as you happened by?)

Yeah, what about that? Awful convenient that such a thing would be playing as I happened by. Never mind the power still being on, but the fact that the station was a news station, giving me the precise details of God knows what? All very convenient indeed.

"…stop them by destroying the brain…"

What do you expect if such a thing is true? The Price is Right? I imagine all *channels are covering it. All channels are now news channels.*

I've got *to still be asleep. Got to. This is simply—*

"…bitten, then you must amputate and cauterize *immediately* under risk of infection and becoming one of…"

—impossible.

(So what are you going to do?)

I'm going to find someone and get some fucking answers. I know I heard someone in my room.

(You were probably dreaming.)

Oh, that part *was a dream??? Someone* is *in this hospital. I'm finding them.*

I spot an elevator. Will it even work?

(Why not? Place is curiously still powered up, no reason the elevator should be exempt from it.)

I press the button for the lobby floor, and it glows. Guess the elevator isn't exempt, though I wonder whether I should take the stairs instead. If the power *does* decide to call it quits, I don't want to be trapped in an elevator when it does.

I look to my right, see the stairwell in the distance, and start for it. Just as I do, the elevator dings, the doors slide apart, and the butt of a shotgun is rammed into my chest, taking both my wind and my balance. I go sailing backwards, flat onto my ass. I can't breathe.

"*Say something! Say something now!*" A big black dude is screaming down at me; his shotgun, the hurty part, is now pointed at my head.

"Something now," I manage to say, my breath only slightly back.

The black guy frowns, confused. A second later and his brow comes unscrunched. He lowers his shotgun and offers me both a sly little smile and a hand to help me up.

"Sorry about that," he says, hoisting me to my feet. "Can't be too sure, you know. Not proud to say I used to be a shoot-first, ask-questions-later kind of guy. Shot someone who wasn't infected when all this insanity started. Not sure I'll ever be able to live it down."

I rub my chest, my breath fully back, but I can only nod back at him; what he said, what I've witnessed thus far—the barren hospital, the news on the TV—is still too crazy to comprehend.

A woman appears from behind the big black guy. She's carrying a pistol in her right hand. She's also smoking hot, not the least bit unkempt. Even though the world apparently started going to shit several weeks ago, she seems to have made her appearance priority one. Doesn't make much sense, nor do the odds that the first girl I see is a freaking ten. And lest we forget the token black badass with a conscience. Wonder if he'll be the first to die, too.

(*Why are you analyzing such things? Just be glad they weren't a horde of zombies.*)

I'm still not buying it. It all seems too theatrical.

"What's your name?" she asks me.

"I don't know," I say. And it's the truth. I still can't remember shit.

"You don't know?" the black guy says.

I shake my head. "I woke up in a hospital bed about ten minutes ago. I can't remember much of anything before that."

The black guy and the hot girl exchange a look.

"Head injury?" she proposes to him.

"You mean like amnesia?" he replies.

She nods back.

He shrugs, then turns back to me while still addressing her. "Well, we gotta call him something."

"What should we call you?" she asks me.

I raise both hands. "Wait a sec—just hold on for one second. Before we do introductions, would it be too much to tell me just what the actual fuck is going on?"

"End of the world, chief," the black guy says. "Dead folks are alive and hungry, and we're on the menu."

Pretty witty reply, and more than a little cheesy, considering the supposed circumstances. I all but roll my eyes at him.

"You can't be serious," I say.

"Look around you, chief," he says. "Find it a little odd that you're the only one here?"

"I do, yes. But zombies—"

"Don't believe us then," the girl says. "Stay here and find out for your damned self."

Oh, and she's got attitude to go with those looks, does she? Of course she does. Will we bicker back and forth for a while until we ultimately fall in love?

"Sharon…" the black guy says, shooting her a disapproving glance.

"*What?*"

"Can you blame the guy? Imagine you just woke up to all this—how would *you* react?"

"Whatever," she responds. She then stares hard at me. "You've got two choices: stay here and find out that what we're telling you is the truth the hard way, or come with us and see for yourself."

"Come with you where?" I ask.

"Supply run," the black guy answers. "Medicinal stuff here, then food and water down the block."

"Is it just the two of you?" I ask.

"No," he says, "there's more of us back at the house. Sharon and I handle the supply runs."

"And you are?"

He extends his hand. "Barney."

I shake his hand, then look past him at her. "And I guess that makes you Sharon?"

"Not as dumb as he looks," she mutters.

Okay, come on now—she's laying on this tough-girl act a little thick. It's all I need to make up my mind.

"Well, Barney, Sharon, as much as I appreciate your offer, I think I'd prefer to go it alone." I turn and start back the way I came.

"Wait!" Barney calls to me. "Don't be stupid, man. You won't last five minutes on your own."

I keep walking, hold up a hand, and wave back to them over my shoulder.

"Let him go," I hear Sharon say to Barney. "He'll be dead soon, and then we can call it quits."

Odd thing to say.

Barney apparently agrees. "*What the hell are you doing?*" he asks in a loud whisper. His tone is different than his previous chastising of her, as though she blasphemed or something.

She mutters back a reply I can't make out, nor do I care to. I turn the corner and begin heading down a new corridor, hoping to find another stairwell. I spot one in the distance and head for it…

THE TRACK

Stiles immediately snatched his phone from his breast pocket. The director answered on the first ring and clearly started talking first.

Stiles listened with the rare sight of agitation in his usual stoic manner.

"I don't care if the producer *was* responsible for hiring her," Stiles finally said, "it's *your* job to ensure that actors never break character." He listened some more. "Are you actually *debating* this with me? It is very possible that the pony *did* hear her comment…mmhmm…well, I do hope you're aware that directors and producers are just as likely to find themselves suddenly unemployed as any actor might."

Suddenly unemployed, Angela thought. *Track speak for suddenly unalive.*

"I see…" Stiles went on into the phone. "Well, then for her sake—and *yours*, I'll remind you again—you might want to hope that the hunters lying in wait inside that stairwell *do* put an end to him now. This pony is particularly clever; he's been known to figure a thing or two out, even *with* proper implantation."

Stiles hung up. Addressed the table.

"The director is confident that Calvin is heading to the stairwell. There are two hunters waiting for him there, two hunters with exceptionally high success rates. The director believes that the waiting hunters will make this little…" Stiles spiraled a hand, searching for the word, the word soon arriving with clear distaste on his lips. "…*snafu* ultimately irrelevant."

Eleanor Flynn had shot Angela a smug little glance the moment Stiles had announced the high success rate of the two hunters lying in wait for Calvin; one of them or perhaps both were surely hers. And though she would never give Eleanor the satisfaction of showing as much, Angela's pulse quickened upon hearing this fact.

Come on, sexy, prove that director wrong. Prove this cunt Eleanor wrong. If you do, I'll find some way to fuck you silly.

THE SET

The stairwell is one of those emergency exit ones. No elevator nearby. I pause a moment before entering, recalling how Barney and the butt of his shotgun greeted my sternum by the elevator near reception. How Sharon had emerged right after, wielding her pistol and her (*too*) good looks and her (*too*) tough-girl attitude, like some kind of badass heroine from the silver screen, all of that balanced by big Barney and his empathy regarding my salvation, of course. And lest we forget his cheesy line: "Dead folks are alive and hungry, and we're on the menu."

Hard to argue with the empty hospital. Hard to argue with the news on that solitary TV at reception, verifying Barney's cheese. But still—*zombies*?

I open the stairwell door.

A huge guy lunges for me, grabbing me around the neck with both hands, ramming me backwards into the wall. He's foaming at the mouth, snarling, his face is gray, his eyes are gray, he smells like shit, he looks like—wait for it—a fucking zombie.

The guy is impossibly strong. Begins slamming my head against the wall behind me, keen on cracking it wide open, and he's nearly there; one or two more whacks and I'm fucked. It's a familiar (*???*) feeling, like I've been caught with a good punch and approaching dreamland, and only a few more will be enough to put me away for good.

I jam my thumb into his gray (*dead?*) eye, and the zombie cries out. For some reason, my first thought—followed immediately by *who fucking cares?*—is, *can zombies feel pain?*

Evidently they can, because the thing releases his hold on me and clutches its wounded eye. I instinctively follow up with a barrage of punches. Not flailing, schoolyard shots either, but focused, practiced blows, looking for his jaw, hoping to knock him cold. And as my final punch, a left hook Joe Frazier

(*Joe Frazier? Who's that???*)

would be proud of, lands smack on the hinge of its jaw and drops him like a stone, my questions again come fast and woefully out of order on the list of priorities, each one rebuked instantly by what is becoming my common-sense mantra:

Irrelevant question one: *How did I know how to punch like that?*

Common-sense mantra: *Who fucking cares?*

Irrelevant question two: *Can you knock zombies out?*

Common-sense mantra: *Who fucking cares?*

The thing begins to stir at my feet. Panting, I look down at it. Its clothes are tattered shreds. The skin that is visible beneath its clothes is as gray as its face. It begins to moan as it comes to, eyes fluttering. If—*if*—the damn thing is a zombie, what was it the news said?

"*…stop them by destroying the brain…*"

That makes sense. That's how you kill them in nearly every zombie film I've seen.

(*When? When did you see these films? And as* who? *Who were you when you watched them?*)

The zombie is stirring more. Common-sense mantra says its thing, followed by: *Just destroy the fucking brain!*

A blinding flash of white light and I drop to my knees, *my* brains feeling as though they're being destroyed. Something comes back to me in splashes of that white light. A scene from a film. A film I'm sure I've seen, one relevant to my thoughts moments ago about destroying the brain in *nearly* every zombie film I've seen.

The film is *The Return of the Living Dead*. The zombies do not die by having their brains destroyed in that film…

> Actor Thom Mathews after actor Clu Gulager drove a pickaxe into a reanimated body's skull to no avail: *The brain! The brain!*

Clu Gulager firing back: *I hit the fucking brain!* Then Clu Gulager to actor James Karen: *I thought you said if we destroyed the brain, it'd die!*

James Karen, hopelessly shouting back: *It worked in the movie!*

Clu Gulager, angry: *Well, it ain't working now, Frank!*

Finished up by Thom Mathews's hilarious (*and relevant?*) line: *You mean the movie lied?!*

The pain is almost unbearable now. I feel as though I'm about to pass out. An aneurysm of some kind? Is this what landed me in the hospital to begin with? What gave me amnesia? And there's no *who fucking cares?* common-sense mantra this time.

Because I do fucking care.

Because just before I pass out, I see another zombie exit the stairwell.

THE TRACK

"This is getting ridiculous," Eleanor Flynn said. "How many times must we delay a day's event because of this pony's inability to handle an implant?" She looked at Angela. "You're relatively new here, Miss Thorne, so allow me to enlighten you: we have *never* had a pony experience such difficulties with implantation before."

Angela opened her mouth to reply, but Stiles cut her off:

"Before you reply, Miss Thorne, I must warn you that your conspiracy theories about deliberately botched implantations will not be tolerated."

Angela closed her mouth, shifted her gaze to one of the enormous monitors lining the walls. The entire table did the same. Calvin was still unconscious. The "zombie" hunter he had knocked out was now upright but on wobbly legs, the second zombie hunter that had emerged from the stairwell offering him a shoulder to lean on. Neither one continued their attack. They knew the rules. They would not be paid for attacking a helpless pony.

Soon, Barney and Sharon were on the scene, and though Stiles had muted the sound, it was clear by their body language and gesturing that they were trying to get the story from the second hunter. Trying to determine what their next course of action might be before officially hearing from the director.

Angela eventually splayed her hands, let them flop into her lap. "So, what would you like me to say?"

"What *can* you say?" Eleanor asked. "Your pony is inferior."

"He is? Sure as hell could have fooled me."

"In regards to implantation, he is inferior," Eleanor countered.

"He's never had a single issue with The Stable implantation."

"Yes, and that is far more important than a Cliché implantation, isn't it?"

Someone at the table snickered at Eleanor's sarcasm. A man. Meticulously dressed like the rest. Meticulously groomed like the rest. The one exception to his perfect shell being a small white scar running through his left eyebrow. Angela shot him a look. He smiled back.

"He set us back during his last outing," Eleanor went on. Her gaze then left Angela and fixed on Stiles. "Shall we allow him to set us back yet again, Robert?" Her question was anything but. It was a challenge.

Stiles, while clearly not amused—his stoicism was once again showing the rarest of cracks from Eleanor's impertinence, from the day's mishaps thus far—did what Angela never imagined he would do. He conceded to Eleanor—sort of.

"No, Eleanor," Stiles started calmly, though he would not look at her with his reply; he looked at Angela instead. "We will not allow Miss Thorne's pony to set us back once again."

"Meaning what?" Angela said.

"Calvin has struggled with implantation in the past, this much is true," Stiles began, "but he has always managed to emerge victorious."

Now it was Eleanor who asked: "Meaning what?"

"We wake him," Stiles replied. "Just as we did when he was struggling to wake in the hospital bed. We let the event continue as is."

"And if he doesn't wake?" Eleanor asked. "If his brain is fried?"

"Then so be it." Stiles pulled out his phone. The director answered on the first ring again. "Wake him," Stiles said, then listened, and then replied: "Yes, that should do. Allow him to regain his senses. Remove your actors and place the hunters back in the stairwell."

"Wait a minute," Angela said.

"Hold a moment, please," Stiles told the director. He lowered the phone and looked at Angela. "Miss Thorne?"

"You're going to let the hunter he already knocked out have a crack at him again? Calvin would have finished him off if…" But she suddenly realized the error in her argument and stopped. *Calvin would have finished him off if he hadn't passed out, dammit.*

Stiles read Angela's mind, acknowledged her faulty complaint with a single nod, and then raised the phone again. "As I was saying," he told the director, "place the hunters back in the stairwell. You have ten minutes to wake him." Stiles then locked eyes with Angela as he told both the director and, to an extent, Angela herself: "If he passes out again, call it a day. The pony will be put out to pasture."

Angela took no pleasure in deciphering that last little piece of Track speak.

How ironic, she again thought with no pleasure, that the very thing she'd counted on Calvin for in making her a star at The Track—his unbreakable will—might see him prematurely "retired."

Angela could handle Calvin dying at the hands of a hunter (or could she?), but to be extinguished by word of The Track? By word of Eleanor? Oh, and by word of Tom fucking Neil once *he* found out? And it would be a word; the hands of these inferior cunts seated around her now would never be soiled with dirt in their lifetimes.

Angela could not fathom a greater tragedy should it be.

The table watched as a solitary electrode was placed on Calvin's left temple—a small, dime-sized adhesive that would be activated by remote. When—*if?*—he woke? The electrode would stay attached until removed either by Calvin himself, to which he would receive no answers as to what it was and why it was there, or by a hunter in an ensuing fray.

Stiles sent a text to the director to resume action.

A pause, all eyes in the room on their respective screens, all mouths below those eyes slightly ajar with bated breath, none more so than Angela's, and then Calvin's prone body convulsed once, violently, for a good two to three seconds before going limp again. He did not wake.

A collective exhale of disappointment from the table, save Eleanor Flynn, who smiled. Save the man with the scar running through his left eyebrow, who was the only one to take his eyes off his chosen screen and glance over at Angela, appearing to weigh her reaction with only the mildest of affect.

Angela frowned back at the man. Brought her attention back to Stiles. "Tell the director to hit him again."

"Patience, Miss Thorne," Stiles replied. "Do you want—as Eleanor so eloquently put it—to fry his brain?"

THE SET

I jerk on my bar stool like I've just had one of those unexplained shivers that can hit you even on the hottest of days.

"Whoa—you okay there, brother?"

I turn and look at my friend. He is wearing a Yankees hat. I know he's my friend—my best friend. His name is…I don't remember his name.

"Fine," I say.

"You go away again?" He says this not as a dig, but as a friendly sort of jab from someone who knows me all too well.

"I guess I did," I say.

"Next round's on me," he says.

He waves the bartender over, orders himself a Bombay and tonic, and me a shot of Jim Beam and a lager.

The bartender returns with our drinks. My friend raises his and urges me to do the same. I raise my shot.

"To our brief moment together," he says.

I frown. "Brief?"

He points to a scoreboard-type thing in the sports bar we're in. It's counting down like a New Year's Eve ball drop or something. It's on eight minutes and change.

"Little over eight minutes left, brother," he says. "Drink up."

"Eight minutes left?"

"They gave you ten minutes. Two have almost passed. Drink up."

I do, then chase the shot with my lager. The warmth of the whiskey, the cold of the lager after, it's like sex.

"I'm not sure what's going on," I say. "I don't feel right."

"You're *not* right. You're all kinds of fucked up, my friend."

"I am? How?"

"If you don't know, then I don't know, brother. It's *your* memory that brought me here."

"Wait, wait…if you don't know what *I* don't know, then what's with the whole ten-minute countdown thing? How did you know that if I didn't?"

"My guess? You heard someone mention it while you've been here with me. Kinda like an unconscious eavesdropping, so to speak."

"I'm not following *at all*."

"Again, if I had to guess, I would say you're taking a bit of a snooze right now, voluntary or otherwise. Certain people—please don't ask me who just yet—probably aren't happy about that and said you've got ten minutes to wake your ass up."

"So, you mean whoever said it was likely close by, and my unconscious ear snagged it and brought it here somehow?"

"Sounds good to me."

"Why am I unconscious?"

"Like I said: I don't know if you don't. But once again, if I had to guess—" He taps my forehead gently with his index finger. "I'd say the memory loss is a good indicator that someone got in there and did some scrambling."

"You mean like brain damage?"

"Maybe—but not in the tragic accident kind of way. This ten-minute time limit bullshit going on? I'd say that qualifies as enough intrigue to give my doubts merit, wouldn't you?"

"I guess. I just want to remember."

"I'll help as best I can, brother. And if I may yet again make a guess? I'd say that jolt you got a few minutes ago—what they're probably using to try to wake you up—inadvertently unscrambled a few things."

"You think?"

"It certainly brought you here with me." He then flicks the brim of his Yankees cap. "Made you remember my team." He points to my empty shot glass and half-full lager. "Made you remember you like whiskey and beer." He then raises his own glass and wiggles it, ice tinkling. "And it made you remember that mine's a Bombay and tonic. Cheers for that, by the way. If you had me drinking something like tequila—"

"I remember zombies," I blurt.

Both of his eyebrows go up midsip. He swallows and says: "Alrighty then. What about zombies?"

I can't tell whether he's placating me or not.

Then that would mean you're placating yourself, stupid. The clock's ticking; keep talking.

"It sounds crazy to say, but I think I was *fighting* one. I survived, though. I knocked it out. I never knew zombies could be knocked out."

"If anyone could do it, you could."

"What's that supposed to mean?"

"It means you're a bad motherfucker."

"I am?" I pause a moment as the memory (and, thus, *his* memory; the explanation for his knowledge of my fighting prowess) returns. "I did hit him with some punches like I'd…like I'd done it before. Like I've had some decent training or something."

He smiles. "Looks like the surface has officially been scratched."

I shake my head. "But beneath that surface…it's so fucking deep. I still don't know your name, let alone my own."

He orders me another shot. A double. "Let's hope they zap you again, but until they do: drink. You like to drink. It's always been one of your Achilles' heels. I know that much about you; you know that much about yourself. Familiarity might loosen a few things until that next zap."

"What's my other Achilles' heel?"

"*Drink.*"

I do. It goes down a bit rougher than the first, but it's still like sex.

Like rough sex.

Like fun sex.

Rough, fun sex.

Amazing fucking rough, fucking fun sex…

A scene, silhouetted and blurred in my mind's eye, suddenly appears, filmed in an abstractness that doesn't need immediate clarity to convey its insane eroticism. It's something I can just as much feel, almost smell, fucking *taste*.

"A woman," I say. "A woman is my other Achilles' heel."

"Breaking out the pick and shovel now," he says.

"Booze and a woman I get. But *zombies?*"

"It's all related somehow. But we need to figure it out soon." He gestures towards the scoreboard. Five minutes left.

THE TRACK

"Hit him again," Angela said.
 Stiles pulled out his phone. Ordered the director to do so again.

THE SET

Another jolt and I almost fall off my bar stool. A bouncer approaches me.

"You're cut off," the big lump says.

"He's fine," my friend says to the bouncer.

The bouncer grabs my friend's shoulder. "Was I talking to you?"

An urge comes on like a switch. An urge to protect my friend's very life if need be because…because I've done it before?

"Don't touch him," I say to the bouncer.

He turns back to me. "And just what the fuck are you—?"

I headbutt the guy, and he drops like he's dead, nose pissing blood.

Nobody in the bar seems to blink, like it's some kind of Wild West shit where a dude being dropped on the spot is an everyday thing.

My friend smiles and casually sips his Bombay and tonic. "See? Bad motherfucker."

I immediately recall another time where I headbutted a guy in mid-sentence while he was trying to talk tough. It was outside a bar this time, not in. I was protecting a woman. *The* woman? I glance at the scoreboard. Four minutes.

"Okay," I begin quickly, "let's do some math here. I like to drink. It's my Achilles' heel. I can remember that. And this woman, she's my other Achilles' heel, yes? That means both are bad news, yet I want them all the same."

"Keep going."

"I clearly know how to fight. I remember fighting a guy in a parking lot for this girl. She *knows* I can fight. Then I find myself fighting—and this one is muddy as fuck—a freaking zombie. That last one makes zero sense."

"Do you believe in zombies?"

"No…I mean—*no*. But this thing…there was an empty hospital"—*power and water curiously still on after several weeks*—"and there were these two survivors"—*big black guy with the predictable big heart; tough-talking, way-too-hot-under-the-circumstances girl who was overdoing her whole shtick*—"looking for supplies, but it all seemed so…"

"Yes?"

"…contrived."

"Contrived as in staged?"

"*Yes*. I remember it now. There was even something the girl said. It made no sense at the time, but now it's starting to. When I refused their help and wanted to go it alone, she said, 'Let him go; he'll be dead soon, and then we can call it quits.'"

"Now we're really getting somewhere. Think this is your first dance?"

"Huh?"

"Being under the bright lights."

"I don't know. My gut says no. But who's the production for? Who's staging it?"

"One of the bigger questions that needs answering. My guess—*our* guess—is that it's the Achilles' heel who knows what you're capable of."

I look at the scoreboard. Three minutes.

"I need more than another drink. I need another shock to the brain, to help me remember more." I close my eyes and concentrate, willing the shock to come.

"Something tells me someone else is controlling that, my friend. My suggestion is to find a way to do it yourself."

I open my eyes. "How?"

"If you remember anything when you leave here, I would try to remember that. Remember it and then find a way."

Two minutes left.

"It's all too much. What do I do, man?"

"Well, first I would suggest waking up before that timer goes off. Something tells me that's pretty damned important. Second, I suggest you give that Achilles' heel what she wants. Give the best damn performance that only you can and start fucking up some serious shit."

"You're telling me to do what she wants?"

"Consider the alternative. You lay down and something tells me this will be our last cocktail together. We got some decent answers on this little trip of yours, man. You survive this performance and perhaps more answers will come."

"And if I wake up and don't remember a thing?"

One minute.

"I got faith in you, brother. And I know I'll be seeing you again in this bar very soon for another cocktail so we can figure *all* of it out. Love you, man. Now wake the fuck up."

A final jolt *does* send me off the bar stool. I'm flat on my back, next to the bouncer I KO'd. I look up at my friend, who's looking down at me, smiling, raising his glass to me as though saying goodbye. His image begins to fade. My surroundings begin to fade.

"Keep it with you, brother," his fading image says to me. "Remember everything, and go give them one hell of a fucking show."

THE TRACK

"He's awake," someone at the table blurted.

"So he is," Stiles said.

"For now," Eleanor said. "If he passes out again, he's going out to pasture."

"I'm well aware of what I said, Eleanor," Stiles said. "As, I'm sure, is Miss Thorne."

Angela smiled at the two, the way one smiles at someone who has taken a passive-aggressive dig at them in public. "Well aware," she said.

Stiles said: "Well, then without further ado…"

THE SET

I'm awake. The bar is gone. My friend is gone. Best part? I'm able to *know* that the bar and my friend are gone. Because I remember. I remember every damn thing we talked about.

So what now?

In my friend's voice (I can recall it clear as day), I get a response, though technically, as we discussed in the bar, it is a response to myself. My head, his voice.

(*For starters, I would say get off your back before the "zombies" return.*)

I get to my feet, a bit unsteady, like a fighter rising off the canvas from a good punch. And I know this personally because I've experienced it before. Remembering shit is cool.

I turn towards the stairwell. They had the element of surprise on their side last time. Now I do.

(*My man.*)

I inch towards the stairwell door and stop. Another memory flashes. Not of the serious type I've been dealing with, but a quick, transitory one of something seen and subconsciously registered and only returning just now to be full acknowledged.

A fire axe. Encased in glass and on the wall behind me.

Whether I did see it the first time around, or just saw it now as I was getting to my feet, common-sense mantra (now in my friend's voice) did its thing:

(*Who fucking cares?*)

Do hospitals have fire axes encased in glass like this?

(*This hospital, or whatever the hell you want to call it, does. Probably put there on purpose to give the audience a better show should you spot it.*)

And then, of course:

(*Who fucking cares? Just grab it.*)

I go to the case, shield my eyes, and drive my elbow through the glass, shattering it on the first go. I take the axe. Its weight feels good in my hands.

I approach the stairwell again, but I will not unwittingly open it like a human bull's-eye as I did last time.

I step off to one side of the door, crouch down, reach up with one hand for the long steel crossbar that is the door's handle, and simultaneously push down on the bar and shove open the door with as much strength as I can muster from my awkward position.

The "zombie" rushes out on cue, snarling, roaring, the works. The act is fleeting, though. With no victim dead ahead, as he'd expected, he drops the act and freezes, confused.

(*All very normal zombie behavior.*)

Now, many might have expected me to say something cool just then, like *Behind you, pal*, and then wait for him to spin with shock before I buried the axe in his head. I know the "audience" would have loved it.

Only I don't do that shit. "Fair fight" is an oxymoron to me.

I simply come up from behind him and bury that axe into the back of his head with everything I've got, dropping him like a sack of shit, the axe leaving my hands and going with his descent I buried it so deep.

Face down on the tiled floor, axe in his head, its handle standing tall like the pump to a well, he begins to convulse violently. A circle of blood grows around his head by the second.

(*BOOM!*)

No champagne yet. I remember a second waiting.

Like the aforementioned well pump, I crank down on the handle like it's just that, and wrench the axe free. This causes more convulsing, more blood.

I turn back towards the door, expecting the second to charge on out, but apparently he got the memo on what the audience wants and is keen on giving it to them: he's right there, in my face. Fucker had snuck up behind me and was waiting for me to turn around. He robs the audience of a clever quip

(*it would be too un-zombie-like*)

but damn if I don't see the faintest of smirks on his rotted

(*made up*)

face.

First time around, I had stuck my thumb into one of their eyes. A million bucks says this is the same guy, because not only does his eye look jacked up, but he immediately goes for *my* eyes, clamping onto my head with both hands, ramming me back against the wall, digging his thumbs in.

The pain is the whole world. I jerk my head to one side so his thumbs are no longer raping my eyes, but he is not so easily deterred. He continues to try to gouge. Eye for an eye was never so fucking apt.

My instinct is to fire hooks and uppercuts around and up through his outstretched arms, hoping to find his jaw. This instinct does not come to fruition, as the axe still clutched tight in both my hands from panic prevents it.

(*Champagne problems.*)

Indeed.

I hoist, not the blade, but the spike on the opposite end of the axe up and between the guy's legs and bury that spike into his groin.

The guy screeches like some kind of wild bird and instantly backs away, the axe once again leaving my hands, the spike rooted deep and going with him, the handle hitting the floor and dragging along the tiles as he staggers back. No well-pump analogy this time, but how about a giant wooden dick scuffing those tiles? A flaccid one at that.

The guy looks down incredulously at his new wooden member, seemingly afraid to touch it and pull it

(*ha!*)

free for fear of making the pain worse.

Again, a nice little quip would be great right about now—something dick-related, of course—but again, I don't play that game. I simply stroll towards him, load up, and throw an overhand right to his jaw like I'm trying to bust through cement.

I actually *hear* his jaw break, like kindling over one's knee, and he's asleep before he hits the deck. Still strangely calm, I go to him, wrench the axe free, raise it up overhead, and bury it—spike end again—between his eyes.

He too convulses. He too has a lovely circle of blood now growing around his head.

(*Look at you playing the part.*)

Huh?

(*Destroying both their brains?*)

I guess I did, didn't I?

The two "survivors" burst on the scene, guns drawn. I go to pull the axe from the dude's head, but his head comes off the ground with it and I have to step on his face to finally jerk it free. I then spin towards the two of them, axe raised, ready for anything.

"*Whoa, whoa!*" the big black guy says—*what the hell was his name? Barney?* — lowering his shotgun and extending a mollifying palm. "It's cool, man, it's cool…"

The girl—*Sharon?*—checks the damage I inflicted, her tough-girl scowl ever present.

"He get 'em?" Barney asks her.

She nods over her shoulder. "He got 'em."

"Good job, man," Barney says to me.

I say nothing.

Sharon joins Barney's side. "Do you believe us now?" she says.

"No," I say flatly.

The stairwell door bursts open behind us. Three more zombies rush out. Sharon raises her gun and fires off three shots, each one hitting a zombie dead-center, between the eyes. All three drop hard.

I turn back towards Sharon. Her gun is still high and ready. Her face is still Clint Eastwood cool.

"How about now?" she says.

Three shots, three zombies, three *moving* zombies, each shot smack between the eyes? No fucking way. That is definitely some Hollywood bullshit right there—everybody is suddenly a master marksman during a zombie apocalypse.

"Well, let's see," I say. I go over to one of the zombies she shot. It's a male zombie. There's a clear bullet hole in his forehead. There's blood leaking out of the hole. I bend over him and place two fingers to the side of his neck and…voila! A pulse.

"What are you doing?" she asks behind me.

I stand upright and face her. "He's got a pulse. Strange. Even before you shot him, you'd think he wouldn't have a pulse, what with him already being dead and all."

Sharon and Barney exchange an odd glance.

"But who knows, right?" I say. "Better be a hundred percent sure he's dead. Hang on a sec, I'll chop his head off."

The zombie springs to life. Not in the *Grrr…I'm not really dead, and I still want to eat you!* kind of way, but in the *Holy fuck, please don't chop off my fucking head!* kind of way.

"Well, would you look at that?" I say and raise my axe overhead.

The zombie holds up both hands and cries out: "*Don't!*"

I smile and lower the axe. Approach him again and touch his forehead, the bullet hole. His frightened state allows me to do so without resistance. I peel off the hole. It's a squib with some kind of foam latex special-effect thingy covering it. The thing has a small thin wire attached to it that runs the length of his torso and disappears into his pants pocket. I go fishing into that pocket, and again his shocked state offers no resistance. I pull out a small square transmitter and study it up close, the squib now dangling from the transmitter on that small thin wire like a fishing lure.

"Very cool," I say. "Movie magic."

Barney and Sharon say nothing. They don't need to; their faces say it all: *not in the script*.

I toss the transmitter away and head towards the other two zombies, who, bless them, are still in character, playing dead.

"Why don't we see if these two are in on the fun as well, yeah?" I raise the axe again. One of them, a woman this time, opens an eye a slit, and then both eyes pop wide, and she too raises both arms in the air and cries out: "*NO!*"

I laugh and lower the axe. The third zombie, another male, opens his eyes, sits up and blinks stupidly.

THE TRACK

"He's on to us again!" Eleanor said.

"He was on to us in the last one," Angela replied. "I say let it play."

Eleanor looked at Stiles.

Stiles looked at Angela.

"Agreed," Stiles said. "Let it play."

THE SET

I drop the axe and approach Sharon. "Let me see your gun," I say.

"Why?"

I flick my chin past her shoulder, hinting something is behind her. She turns, and I snatch her wrist, pulling the pistol free.

"*Hey!*"

I point the gun at her. She backs up. I fire three shots into her chest. She screams, but remains very much intact.

I tuck the gun filled with blanks into my waistband. "Just making sure."

I face Barney now. "What about you, partner? That loaded with bullshit too?"

Barney points the barrel of the shotgun at my face. "Care to find out, *partner?*"

I raise both hands as though yielding to his threat. "Cool, cool…"

He lowers the gun.

My hands still raised in a submissive gesture, I drop a hammer fist blow down onto the bridge of his nose. He instantly drops the shotgun and clutches his shattered nose with both hands. I bend quickly, snatch up the shotgun, cock it, and aim it at his chest.

Whether he could just make it out through the watery eyes we all get from a good crack on the nose, or whether he couldn't see shit but heard me cock the thing,

(*who fucking cares?*)

he clearly knows that he's about to get the Sharon treatment and takes his bloodied hands away from his busted nose and starts pleading with them.

"It's real! It's real!"

I point the shotgun at the ceiling and pull the trigger. The blast jolts me, and the fiberglass tiles overhead explode and begin sprinkling down on me like snow.

"So it is," I say, wiping that fiberglass snow from my face and—hello?—what's this? I pluck an odd little thing from my left temple. I study it. It looks like a tiny watch battery.

(*The receiver they were using to shock you?*)

I'll buy that.

(*Keep it.*)

Would like to find the remote they were using to induce that shock.

(*Never hurts to ask.*)

"What is this?" I say, brandishing the watch battery thingy.

"Electrode," Sharon says. "You passed out earlier. They were using it to try to wake you."

"Who's 'they?'"

She says nothing.

"It's wireless," I say. "Where's the remote?"

"They have it."

"Again, who's 'they?'"

And again, she says nothing.

"You're starting to piss me off, guys." I hold up the electrode between my thumb and index finger. "When they were zapping me with this thing, it was helping me get my memory back. I'd like to get more of it back."

"We don't have the remote," Sharon says. "Swear to God."

(*Move on for now.*)

I pocket the electrode and do move on.

Why did Barney's gun have real bullets, but Sharon's blanks?

(*I'm guessing two reasons: hers was for show, to sell you on the idea of zombies and that she was indeed a badass. His? My guess was that it's not unlike the axe—something strategically planted for you to use if need be. At least the bastards are giving you a fighting chance.*)

The bullet-hole zombies behind me are now on their feet, exchanging dumbfounded looks and periodically murmuring and shrugging to one another.

"So, what now? Unlike those three"—I gesture to the bullet-hole zombies with the shotgun; one of them flinches—"these two"—I gesture down at the two I dispatched—"were clearly trying to hurt me. Was it just them, or is there more?"

Barney and Sharon hesitate. I cock the shotgun and aim it at them.

"There's more!" Sharon cries. Her tough-girl act is well and truly gone. Still smoking hot, though.

"Great. Tell me where."

"They're everywhere," Barney says. His nose is a mess. Blood drips from it onto his chin and shirt.

I put the shotgun on him again. "Dude, if you keep trying to sell me on that shit, I'm gonna take your mind off that broken nose by blowing your dick off."

(*Nice! Who said you couldn't manage a quip now and then?*)

"No," Barney says quickly, "I don't mean it like that. I mean that they're positioned all over. I don't know exactly where. They're ordered to show up at different times."

"How many more?"

"There are seven on contract, I think. Well, five now."

"*On contract?* Ooh, this just gets better and better. What about you guys? You on contract too?"

Barney and Sharon hesitate again before looking up at the ceiling, about five feet behind me.

I turn and look too. I see nothing but a ceiling with tiles I haven't blown to bits. No, wait—that's a lie. I see a small, glass dome. I might have thought it an alarm system if they both hadn't looked at it like students waiting on teacher.

(*Or actors waiting on director.*)

"What?" I say. "What's up there? Is that my audience? No—it's the puppeteer, isn't it?" I wave at the glass dome. "Hey, sweetheart? You enjoying the show? What do you say we stop fucking around and you send me the remaining five?"

THE TRACK

All eyes fell on Angela.

"What?" she said.

"He seems to have recalled quite a bit," Stiles said. "Not only has he figured us out again, but he seems to recall *you*, Miss Thorne. Our attempts to shock him back to consciousness clearly brought some of his memory back."

"You don't know that," Angela countered. "He never said my name. 'Puppeteer?' 'Sweetheart?' It's broad. And if even he does remember, so what? When it's over, if he survives, I'll collar him, and all will be erased."

"He figured us out in the last one, but the performance from our staff was seen to the end," Eleanor said. "All actors have broken character. We have nothing now."

"I say it's still salvageable," Angela said. "Calvin seems more than willing to give us a show."

Eleanor shook her head. "Such a mess—*again*. I say we shut it down."

"I say you try shutting your fucking mouth for a change."

Eleanor slammed her fist on the table.

"Miss Thorne…" Stiles began, displeased.

Angela didn't let him finish. "My logic is sound, and you know it. Let it play out. When it's done, he'll either be dead, or I'll collar him."

"I agree with Miss Thorne," the man with the scar in his left eyebrow said. "I say we let it play out."

Angela frowned the man's way for the second time that day, more of a curious than annoyed frown this time. She brought her attention back on Stiles, her steely gaze waiting.

"And his request for sending all five at once?" Stiles asked.

All five at once. No way could her Calvin survive such an onslaught. Even with the shotgun and axe.

Unbreakable will, she then thought. The very thing that saw her beloved Calvin through chaos. The very thing that also threatened his place in The Stable for fainting spells and supposed difficulties in handling implantation. *One who thrives on chaos cannot have order. Implantation. Stable. The whole damn Track? Order doesn't come much cleaner. And somewhere deep down, my man knows it.*

Let him thrive.

"Give him what he wants," she said. She was not aware that she was smiling.

THE SET

I approach Sharon, shotgun leading the way. I gesture to her waist, where a black fanny pack hangs. "Got any real bullets in there?"

"Why?"

"Because five men are about to storm this hospital, hell bent on killing me. I would very much like another gun with real bullets, please."

She looks at Barney. He wipes blood from his chin. "Just give it to him," he says.

She unzips her fanny pack, produces a clip, and hands it to me. I pop the clip of blanks, shove it in my back pocket, and then load the clip with real (I hope) bullets.

"Gotta make sure," I say, pointing it at her.

"*They're real!*" she cries.

I smile, point the gun at the ceiling, and fire. No crazy explosion followed by fiberglass snow like with the shotgun, but it's clearly the real deal; there's a tidy little hole in the tile I shot this time, this one offering only the mildest of flurries.

"Beautiful," I say and point the gun at Barney. "How many points of entry are there in this place?"

They exchange another look.

I sigh. "Guys, can you please stop with all the hesitancy shit? You're no longer on the clock. Your gig is done. You can either help me, or I can shoot you both now and do it on my own. Personally, I'd rather not waste the ammo. Up to you, though."

"Three," he says.

"Three? This hospital only has three points of entry?"

"It's not a real hospital. Just supposed to look like one. We weren't supposed to be here long. We were supposed to take you out of here if you survived the first attack by the stairwell."

"Stairwell—that's one point of entry. I saw another east of the elevator. I'll assume that's the second. Which would then make the elevator the third. How am I doing?"

"Spot on," Barney says.

"How about floors?" I ask. "How many floors?"

"Just two," Barney says. "Again, it's not a real—"

I hold up a hand. "Yeah, yeah, I got it. So, two floors, three points of entry. I'm assuming we're on the second floor?"

He nods.

"Okay. What say we go eliminate one of those points of entry right now?"

I start down the hall towards the elevator, shotgun over one shoulder, pistol tucked in my waistband, feeling, well, yeah—feeling pretty fucking cool. In the grand scheme of things, I have no idea what is going on, but that's some forest shit for another time. Right now, I'm taking it tree by tree, and five of those trees are heading my way, none of their intentions good.

I arrive at the elevator and am surprised to see that Barney and Sharon have followed me.

"You guys aren't getting any stupid ideas, are you?" I ask them.

"Like what?" Barney says.

"Like trying to get the jump on me while my back is turned. Payback for busting your nose."

"You said you'd shoot us if we didn't help," he says, his voice now coming out congested as though he has a cold, courtesy of said broken nose. "It's like you said: Our gig is finished. We're off the clock. We have nothing to gain by jumping you."

"Fair enough. Just mind your p's and q's."

I aim the shotgun at the elevator's control panel. "Let's just eliminate one of those points of entry now, shall we?"

The familiar ding of the elevator stops me. The number two above the elevator door glows. Hum of the elevator moving.

"They aren't stupid enough to use the elevator, are they?" I ask, more myself than them.

I raise the shotgun again and blast the control panel. Sparks and metal fly. The glowing number two above the elevator dies. The hum dies.

Shouts and curses from within the elevator, clear as a bell, hinting they were close to arrival when I derailed them. Now arguing from within the elevator's carriage: *"Open it!" "How?" "Move! Get out of the fucking way!"*

Grunts of labor now as the elevator doors are pried open manually from within.

There are two inside, both made up as zombies, each busy pulling open their half of the elevator door as far as it will go. They are too busy in their efforts to immediately notice me looming over them.

Yes, looming.

The carriage had stopped a few feet from floor level, their heads at my knees. If they wanted out, they would have to climb out.

I squat down. "Gentlemen," I say.

They look up at me, startled.

I gesture towards their zombie getups. "Still in character, huh? Got to admire your commitment to the craft. Or maybe no time for a wardrobe change?"

(*Another zinger! Is it getting easier?*)

It kinda is!

I aim the shotgun at one of their heads.

How about this?

"That's a wrap, boys," I say and blow the first guy's head clean off.

(*HA!*)

The headless zombie falls back into the carriage wall and slumps onto his ass, sitting upright, the stump of his neck spouting great arcs of blood that decorate the interior of the carriage, his friend included. His friend is also wearing what's left of the guy's head. *Real* makeup.

"He's got a gun!!!" the second screams—a likely warning to the remaining three in hopes that they are in earshot.

I pump the shotgun, expel the empty shell, and blow the second's head clean off as well.

(*Look at you still playing the part. Four dead zombies, all four brains destroyed.*)

I smile and turn back towards Sharon and Barney. Their faces are an easy read: guy just blew off the heads of two men, is flecked with blood and brain (some of it did hit me, mostly my pants, but I did feel a light misting on my face), and is now facing us with a wry little smile? Lunatics *wish* they could project such a show.

"Two down," I say to them, pumping the shotgun and expelling another shell. "One point of entry down as well. Do me a favor and go check the stairwell?" I gesture to the stairwell east of the elevator.

Neither one moves.

I raise the shotgun on them. "Please?"

Both spin and head for the stairwell. I quickly bend and lay the shotgun on the floor. Pull the pistol from my waist, pop the clip, stuff it into my back pocket, pull the clip of blanks from my other back pocket, slam it home, and then pick the shotgun back up.

"Anything?" I call to them.

They return from the stairwell.

"Not as far as we can tell," Barney says.

"Yeah, for now," I say. "Do me a favor and keep watch on it. I'm going for the other stairwell." I go to hand Sharon the pistol. She reaches for it, and I pull it back. "The gig is over, yes? You have nothing to gain by turning on me?"

Sharon quickly nods. I hand her the gun, turn my back on her, and slowly start for the other stairwell.

Wait for it…

Click of the pistol's hammer being cocked behind me. "Turn around."

I slowly turn. Sharon is pointing the gun at me.

"What are you doing?" Barney asks her.

"It's like he said," she replies, "the gig is over. We broke character. You know what happens to actors who break character, Dean."

Dean? I liked Barney so much better.

"Ashley, don't do this," Barney says.

Ashley's not bad, I guess. Sharon's better.

"You'll thank me for it," she says. Then to me: "Put down the shotgun."

I do.

She then takes a cautious step back, gun staying on me as she looks over her shoulder towards the little glass globe in the ceiling that is adjacent to the stairwell. Towards another camera. Another camera that I had already spotted.

"I want to make a deal!" she shouts to the camera. "Send the remaining three to the east stairwell. I'll keep him here. What happens after that happens, but I want a promise that me and Dean get out of this alive."

"What about the three by the west stairwell?" I ask. "The ones with the fake bullet holes?"

"Fuck 'em," she says. "Don't know them."

"That's cold."

She turns her head back towards the camera. "We have a deal?"

Barney's—sorry, *Dean's*—pocket vibrates. He pulls a cell phone. Reads a text.

"It's the director. He wants assurance that his life will be spared too for this mess. The producer's life too. He's contacting The Track now."

The Track?

THE TRACK

Stiles, cell phone muted, conveyed the proposal to the table.

The man with the scar in his left eyebrow was first to speak. "I say why not?"

"Loose ends," was all Stiles said.

The man with the scar shrugged. "And what's to stop any other director, producer, or actor we have under employment from flapping their gums about what we do?"

"Incentive," Stiles said. "Their pay is exceptional."

"Okay, incentive," the man with the scar said. "Dare I say the urge to live is a greater incentive than money?"

Stiles looked at Angela. "Miss Thorne?"

"Honestly?" Angela said. "I couldn't care less about anyone but Calvin."

"And yet the deal Ashley is proposing is to serve your pony up on a platter in exchange for their lives."

Did no one else notice Calvin's little switcharoo trick with the pistol's ammo? she thought. *They had to have.*

Or maybe they had noticed and wanted to watch it play out? Even Eleanor, perhaps. After all, what were they doing here? What did it all come down to in the end? Was it not for putting on a good show for this table of depravity she found herself in company with, she most certainly and admittedly not excluded from that company?

Calvin's little switcharoo was the twist in the film they all knew was coming. To leave your seat and exit the theater before seeing such a twist unfold?

Fucking without coming, she mused, biting her lip.

"Give them the deal," Angela said. "Or, hell, *say* you'll give them the deal. What you do afterwards is up to you."

Stiles offered Angela the faintest of smiles. She offered one back. Two psychopaths talking without talking.

Stiles turned to Eleanor. "Eleanor, you're curiously quiet."

"I have nothing to say that I already haven't." She would not look at Angela.

Stiles leaned forward, addressing the table as a whole. "Can we say we're in agreement then? Ashley's, the director's, and the producer's deal is a go?"

The table nodded and murmured in unison.

Stiles unmuted his phone and brought it to his ear.

THE SET

Barney's phone vibrates again. "It's a go," he says. "They're sending them."

Ashley—oh hell, you know what? I'm just gonna keep calling them Sharon and Barney—sighs relief.

Sounds echoing from the base of the stairwell—heavy door slamming, footsteps thumping their way on up.

"Sorry about this," she says to me. "Dog eat dog, you know?"

"Totally understand," I say.

She frowns a little. "You're awfully cavalier."

I shrug. "I don't think you have it in you to shoot a real person."

"I won't have to. They'll be here any minute."

"And if I take the gun from you during that brief interim?"

"Then I will shoot you."

"No, you won't."

"Try me."

"Okay."

I step towards her. She fires, the bitch. Part of me really didn't think she would have it in her. But then she did give zero fucks about the poor zombie actors by the west stairwell.

No bullet hits me, of course, and for a moment she looks as though she thought she'd missed (lovely irony considering the character she was previously portraying), and she fires again and, of course, hits nothing again. Fires again.

"Uh-oh," I say, and though I'm not proud of it, I whip a short little right hook into the side of her jaw and drop her cold.

I bend, pick up the pistol, pop the blanks, go into my back pocket, pull the second clip, and load the real thing.

Barney looks on with equal parts shock and confusion.

I stuff the pistol into my waistband again, bend to pick up the shotgun. Echoes of those pounding footsteps in the stairwell growing louder. Almost here.

I look at Barney. "You might want to get out of the way, Barney."

He does.

The stairwell door opens. All three (and yes, they too are still made up as zombies) rush towards me, two literally skidding to a stop on the tiled floor when they notice my shotgun on them.

I blow a hole in the first one's chest, sending him flat on his back, very dead.

I pump the shotgun, expel the shell, and go to blow a hole in number two.

Click!

"Fuck." I pump it again. Fire again. *Click!* again.

Zombie two actually grins and rushes forward. And I happily meet that grin with the butt of my shotgun, ramming it into his face, taking him off his feet and onto the deck where he lay, still grinning (though technically it's more of a grimace) with no front teeth.

I toss the shotgun aside and pull the pistol from my waist, keen on emptying it into zombie three.

Zombie three, however, is keen on no such thing. His arms are in the air; any blood lust he might have had is gone.

"I'm out," he says. "I'm done."

"You're *what?*"

I look at Barney.

"Hunters are allowed to bow out of an event at any time if they so choose," he says.

I can only stare back at him.

He shrugs. "Apparently it's frowned upon, but it's the rules."

"I'm out," zombie three says again. Then, towards the stairwell, towards the little glass dome in the ceiling, hands still in the air: "I'm out!"

"Like fun you are," I say, step towards zombie three, and fire three shots.

And miss all three.

SEE?!

I close in on him and keep firing, the bullets eventually landing—one in his leg; one in his gut; and then a final one in his chest before the gun clicks empty. I must have fired the damn thing a million times from like five fucking feet away and only got him with three shots.

Fucking stupid movie cliché…

Zombie two begins to groan behind me. I turn and head back towards him. Raise my foot high into the air and begin stomping on his head until I hear something crack and feel something give. His body goes rigid with a seizure, and I give him one final stomp for good luck. If he's not dead, his brain is.

Panting, I turn and face Barney, then gesture down to Sharon. "When she wakes up, tell her I'm sorry."

He nods.

"So, what now?" I say. "That's it, right? They're all—"

THE TRACK

The room watched Calvin collapse to the floor, unconscious. Angela held the thumb drive-sized "collar" before the table for all to see, her thumb hovering over the single button she'd just pressed.

"There, you see?" she said. "We got a good show, and now Calvin will remember none of it."

"Assuming he doesn't recall the particulars jogged loose from our attempts at waking him earlier," Stiles said.

"The collar resets all, doesn't it?" Angela said. "When he wakes, he'll just be another inmate in the stable."

"I hope so, Miss Thorne—for your sake."

Angela nodded. Then: "Sorry about your three hunters, Eleanor," she said. "Wait—I suppose it's four now, isn't it?"

Eleanor appeared to swallow bile, stood, and left.

"Miss Thorne…" Stiles said.

Angela nodded an apology and stood to leave as well. Other members of The Track followed suit and began filing out of the room. Some stayed to watch the "bonus features" still playing on all screens: the director and the producer showing up on set, helping Barney wake Sharon, the three zombies by the west stairwell now on the scene, fidgeting and chatting nervously with one another, cleaners showing up moments after, guns drawn, shooting all seven participants in the day's botched cliché multiple times until they stopped moving.

When more cleaners arrived on the scene with body bags, and there was no more carnage to see, the remaining members left, their sordid minds pleasantly stuffed for the day.

THE STABLE

The cool officer taps his baton on the bars of my cell. "Almost time for lights-out, Twenty-two."

I lift Pele off my chest, get up from my cot, and gently lay him back down on my pillow. The little bugger never stirs throughout. In the throes of an awesome dream about mice and birdies and a mountain of catnip, perhaps.

I approach the bars. The officer is holding what looks like a shopping bag.

"What do you got in there?" I ask.

"Call me Santa Claus," he says.

"Gifts?"

He nods. "A few for you, a few for Pele."

"Why?"

"You don't want them?"

"No, no—I do."

He smiles, reaches into the bag, and pulls out a Styrofoam cup with a plastic lid. "Some more Jim Beam to help you sleep…" He hands it to me through the bars, goes into the bag, and produces a small piece of meat wrapped in plastic wrap, similar to before. "A little snack for Mr. Pele…"

I take the meat, set it on my table with the cup of whiskey, and return to the bars.

"…and finally…" He pulls out what looks to be a…a wadded-up pair of panties?

"What are those?"

"It's what's inside that counts," he says and hands them to me.

I open up the panties and spot a dime-sized thing like a watch battery. It's adhered in the center of a small circle of gauze. One side has a piece of adhesive tape. It looks incredibly familiar, and my head begins to ache.

"What's this?" I ask.

"Open it and see."

"Open it?"

He pulls a small remote from the bag, smiles, and says: "The opener."

"I'm not following at all, man."

He tells me to place what he calls an electrode onto one of my temples. Tells me to then lie down and hit the remote. He assures me the experience will be well worth it.

I'm hesitant, of course, but so far the guy has been ridiculously cool to me and Pele.

"Thanks," I say, then place the electrode, remote, and panties onto the table next to the meat and whiskey.

"Merry Christmas," he says.

"Is it Christmas?"

"Was a joke, Twenty-two."

"Oh." I give a courtesy laugh.

"Lights-out in ten. Sweet dreams, man. I look forward to hearing about your night in the morning." He winks at me and leaves.

I go to my table. Study the electrode for a moment and, then, the panties it was wrapped in. They're damn nice. I bring them to my face and inhale deep—I'm in prison, after all.

Like the electrode, the smell of the panties is familiar. The slightest hint of an enticing body spray coupled with a natural musk that is equally—no, more so—as enticing as the spray. And familiar. Like the body spray, that natural musk (*were they recently worn, and yet to be washed?*) is so damned familiar.

But how could that be? I suppose any woman's natural musk would be enticing to a man in prison, but familiar?

My head continues to ache. I pop the lid on the Styrofoam cup and drink the Beam in an effort to rid myself of it.

The whiskey is gone in less than a minute. My headache on its way, thank God.

And the final gift?

Looking in the mirror above my sink, I attach the electrode to my left temple. I then turn to my cot with both the remote *and* the panties. Don't judge.

I lift Pele off my pillow, lay on the cot, and place Pele on my chest. As before, he never stirs. Mice and birdies and a mountain of catnip.

The whiskey has given me a pleasant little buzz. I smell the panties again, then stuff them under my pillow.

I hold the remote in my hand and stare at it like I'm on a diet and it's a sinful treat.

Why not?

I hit the solitary button on the remote.

As before, the meticulously dressed man with the scar running through his left eyebrow was waiting for Officer Hall the moment Hall exited Calvin's cell block.

And as before, the man with the scar asked the same: "Everything go all right?"

"Yep," Hall said. "Gotta admit, though; part of me wanted to keep those panties for myself." He smiled. "Whose are they?"

And as before, the man with the scar said: "My business; not yours."

Hall only smiled and held out his hand.

The man with the scar handed Hall the ritual envelope filled with cash. "Until next time," he said.

"Until next time," Hall said.

I'm back at the bar. None of it is foreign to me. I remember it like a pleasant memory. Problem is, the stool next to me is empty. My friend is not here to greet me and fill me with both booze and information.

I do see him, though. He's in the distance, by the bar's entrance. The bouncer won't let him in.

I go to rise from my stool and approach, to let the bouncer know that he's with me and that all is cool. If the bouncer has a problem with that, then I'll just knock him the fuck out like I did last time. Nobody in the bar did shit when I did it before.

A hand on my shoulder as I go to rise. A delicate hand, not authoritative. I turn and look into the eyes of one of the sexiest women I've ever seen. She's smiling at me, coquettish and confident. I know her. Like my friend who I'm sure I know, yet can't recall his damn name, I'm a thousand percent sure I know this woman. Her smell especially.

"Take a seat, sexy," she says to me. "Let's talk."

AUTHOR'S NOTE

Thank you so much for reading CLICHÉ: EPISODES ONE, TWO, AND THREE, my friends. Well, it looks as though Calvin's "pony" status is safe again, but for how long? His memory appears to be coming back bit by bit. Shit's about to get real.

Once again, I want to thank you for reading. If you enjoyed CLICHÉ: EPISODES ONE, TWO, AND THREE, I would be extremely grateful if you left a review for it on Amazon. Good reviews are very helpful in the success of a story. It doesn't have to be anything super-long (though feel free to make it as long as you want), just a line or two would be awesome. It would truly mean a lot.

Thanks again, my friends.

Until Calvin meets a Styrofoam cup of Jim Beam he didn't like…

Jeff Menapace

OTHER WORKS BY JEFF MENAPACE

Please visit Jeff's Amazon Author Page or his website for a complete list of all available works!

http://author.to/Jeffsauthorpage

www.jeffmenapace.com

ABOUT THE AUTHOR

A native of the Philadelphia area, Jeff Menapace has published multiple works in both fiction and non-fiction. In 2011 he was the recipient of the Red Adept Reviews Indie Award for Horror.

Jeff's terrifying debut novel BAD GAMES became a #1 Kindle bestseller that spawned four acclaimed sequels, and now the first three books in the series have been optioned for feature film and translated for foreign audiences.

His other novels, along with his award-winning short works, have also received international acclaim and are eagerly waiting to give you plenty of sleepless nights.

Free time for Jeff is spent watching horror movies, The Three Stooges, and mixed martial arts. He loves steak and more steak, thinks the original 1974 *Texas Chainsaw Massacre* is the greatest movie ever, wants to pet a lion someday, and hates spiders.

He currently lives in Pennsylvania with his wife Kelly and their cats Sammy and Bear.

Jeff loves to hear from his readers. Please feel free to contact him to discuss anything and everything, and be sure to visit his website to sign up for his FREE newsletter (no spam, not ever) where you will receive updates and sneak peeks on all future works along with the occasional free goodie!

CONNECT WITH JEFF ON SOCIAL MEDIA

http://www.facebook.com/JeffMenapace.writer
http://twitter.com/JeffMenapace
https://www.linkedin.com/in/JeffMenapace
https://www.goodreads.com/JeffMenapace
https://www.instagram.com/JeffMenapace

FOLLOW JEFF ON BOOKBUB AND AMAZON TO GET THE LATEST ALERTS ON NEW RELEASES!

https://www.bookbub.com/authors/jeff-menapace
https://www.amazon.com/-/e/B004R09M0S

Printed in Great Britain
by Amazon